WEDNESDAY'S CHILD

WEDNESDAY'S CHILD

Amanda Hewett

Book Guild Publishing
Sussex, England

First published in Great Britain in 2006 by
The Book Guild Ltd
25 High Street
Lewes, East Sussex
BN7 2LU

Typesetting in Baskerville by
IML Typographers, Birkenhead, Merseyside

Printed in Great Britain by
CPI Bath

A catalogue record for this book is available from
The British Library.

ISBN 1 85776 984 8

Dedicated to Lucy, wherever you are.

Monday's child is fair of face,
Tuesday's child is full of grace,
Wednesday's child is full of woe,
Thursday's child has far to go,
Friday's child is loving and giving,
Saturday's child works hard for a living,
But the child that is born on the Sabbath day
Is bonny and blithe and good and gay.

Anonymous

Chapter 1

I suppose that you'll want to know how I got myself in here in the first place. Really, it wasn't how I planned it or anything, it just kind of happened, like the way it always rains when you've washed your hair – even if it starts out dead sunny when you head for the shower. You can bet your life that when you head for the door then it will be raining. Well, that was when I was able to head for the door, when I wasn't kept under lock and key every day and night. It certainly makes you appreciate your freedom when it's suddenly taken away from you.

Keeping a journal and writing poetry is the only thing keeping me going, keeping me sane, if that can be said about someone who has spent a week under the watchful eyes of two psychiatric nurses. That means that I was under constant watch for twenty-four hours a day. A potential suicide risk, that was me – that was my recently acquired label. Well, I can't fault them for their observational technique when they did catch me swinging from the big oak tree in the grounds outside … ligature tight around my neck and nearly unconscious (well, maybe I exaggerate a little).

It was a beautiful hot summer's day that Saturday the 17th June and there seemed to be no better time to take my leave from this place. Not that it's a bad place, the newly constructed red-brick building that we are held in is set in the midst of some lovely grounds in the heart of a small village way out in the countryside. It's like a house really with a large room downstairs where we eat and play pool or watch television – but that's only allowed until 8 p.m. Upstairs are the bedrooms, or 'cells', as I prefer to call them.

The village itself where we are situated is so small that there is only one road running through it, with the farms and houses either side of this road but set way back from it. The drive here gave me my first opportunity to even see what the countryside looks like. There sure are plenty of trees here. It seems like I am living in the middle of a jungle, without all the scary animals that roam around and devour you at the first opportunity that they get.

That Saturday I decided that there probably wouldn't be a more pleasant place to die in – at least not one that I would be likely to see. So I gave it what I thought was my best shot, but clearly I wasn't counting on the beady eyes of the others. It was a fellow inmate of mine that alerted the nurse in charge after she saw me tying my jeans belt around my neck as tightly as I could whilst trying to balance on the branch of the tree so that I could jump down at the appropriate moment.

They then stuck me in therapy with some crazy shrink who thinks that he can make it all better, set the world to rights, set me to rights. They are all so busy teaching me the error of my ways, that by the time I am let out of here I'll be a model citizen. That's *their* plan, anyway. As for me, I don't have any plans – just to get out of here after serving my time and return to 'normality' whatever that may be.

'Are you hungry, Lucy?' It is time to eat now – the sandwich trolley has arrived. 'What would you like?' enquired Adam, the head nurse on duty for that day. Each shift there is a different head nurse. Adam is fairly short for a man – about five foot three, aged around thirty with fine dark brown hair which he always keeps cut really short. He has a sense of humour, which is a rare commodity amongst the nurses.

After little thought, 'Tuna' was my unenthusiastic response. It doesn't really matter what you choose to eat in this place, the bread all tastes of cardboard and the fillings are as stale as the bread they fill. So tuna it is, served on the same white plates as always; another day, and another lunch the same as the one yesterday, and no doubt the same as it will be tomorrow.

I took my place at the small faded brown circular dining table with the few other girls and Adam. A nurse is always present at mealtimes to eat with us. We exchanged our views on the sandwiches and nothing was said that day that was any different to what was said the previous day. This alone caused me to feel tired and weary. The dining room itself doubles up into the recreation area, with a great big pool table at the other end of the room. In order to play pool, permission has to be sought from the nurse in charge who will then decide if you are to be trusted with the long wooden cues needed to play the game. The green cloth upon the pool table is the most vivid colour in the otherwise colourless room. The sun comes dancing in through the windowpanes in defiance of the fact that the windows are only able to open a little way. This ensures that no one escapes, or jumps from the building. The windows themselves have draping faded orange curtains either side of them. Each window in the entire building has replica curtains. So much for variety being the spice of life and all that sort of thing.

The nurses' office is also in this same large room, with a big window so that the nurses can watch your every move if they choose to do so. Their view encompasses the dining table, the pool table and the comfy and also faded and battered orange chairs, which are dotted around the edge of the walls. So whatever you are doing, they are supposedly watching. It didn't take too long to get used to the idea of being observed constantly. I say the idea of being observed, because the nurses sometimes sit around drinking their coffee and don't pay any attention to us girls whatsoever. No doubt their interest being caught by their own private affairs if the hushed conversations and references to the consumption of too much alcohol are anything to judge by. There is however a small private sitting room area through the double doors at the far end of this room. With permission we are allowed to spend time in there. It has a really archaic stereo system with reasonable sound quality and a small colour television set. There are a few armchairs and several books.

When I first realised that there was a stereo in the sitting room I was delighted because it meant that I would be able to play my CDs. I had brought some with me, along with a discman, but I just can't get used to wearing headphones or ear pieces.

Although the sitting room area is shielded from the nurses' constant attention I have noticed that with some regularity they do pop in to check up on what is going on. There is no real privacy in this place at all.

Whenever I went into the office – which was on most evenings before bedtime in order to take my medicine – I always noticed some book lying around on the desk. The strangest title I ever saw was on a book called *When Rabbit Howls* – all night I kept thinking of what a howling rabbit would sound like. The nurses seem to read a lot of books while they sat in that office.

Elaine looked at me across the dining table through her hollow empty eyes, devoid of any expression, and I gazed back into that impenetrable darkness, shivering at the thought of what might be behind those dark, almost black eyes. Elaine is thin, skinny in fact, more bones than flesh and tall with it, so she puts one in mind of a skeleton dressed in second-hand rags with her short scraggy hair completing the picture. That's not far from the truth, anyhow, considering the fact that the clothes they give you in here if you haven't got any of your own are mostly from Oxfam and charity shops like that.

4

Most of these guys don't have much in the way of clothes or stuff, but then they don't have much in the way of family either. I guess I'm lucky really – one of the fortunate ones, as I am frequently being reminded by some of the nurses in this place.

'At least you've got parents who care about you, at least your mum and dad love you … Think of everything that you put them through, think of the heartache you cause them …'

That was the trouble with me. On the one hand I didn't think of the trouble and heartache I caused my parents and on the other hand I thought about it so much after I had hurt them that I beat myself up over it repeatedly. An emotional masochist, that's me.

I was expelled from school as a result of my 'disruptive and intrusive' behaviour. I remember clearly the last day that I sat there in the headmaster's office being told how very naughty I was and a disgrace to the school.

'Girls like you shouldn't be allowed to remain here and you won't be for a moment longer' – that was his definitive verdict. 'You are disruptive and intrusive, and on top of that you are personally attacking.'

The thought ran through my head that I would not be able to defend myself if he attacked me so I did not really understand how I came to be the one who was attacking. But I nodded in agreement and repeatedly said sorry. Mr Steadman was unforgiving. Even when he offered me a seat he did it by way of motioning with his large bony hand towards the only available chair. From this I was to understand that I was meant to sit down. I took my place in this low and not to mention uncomfortable beige upholstered chair, trembling from head to foot, and tried to look as sorry as possible in order to halt his anger.

'You are disruptive and intrusive,' he repeated again, pronouncing each syllable clearly and emphatically so that if they had failed to register with me the first time, then they would certainly register the second time. Each word felt like a slap. Each word stung me, pierced me and hurt me. 'You are disrespectful and you are no longer welcome at this school.'

He sat with his legs crossed, scowling at me the whole time he spoke. He wore a sharp blue suit and tie and frowned upon me in my poor – or rather, sloppy – attire of grey jumper and too-short skirt with scuffed shoes, and poorer attitude.

That's really how I ended up here. It was the final straw for my exasperated parents. I had this psychiatric nurse, you see, and he arranged it all with their consent. He came to my house to visit me after Mummy told our family GP that she just couldn't cope with me any longer. She was threatening to put me in care because she could no longer deal with my temper tantrums as she called them. She was probably right, too. I really was extremely naughty and constantly suicidal. Mummy used to let me get away with a lot of tantrums because she loved me and all that, but I tried not to behave badly when my father was at home.

The first time that I met Matthew Richards – that was his name, the psychiatric nurse that I was just telling you about – was when he called at our house to see me at 4 p.m. on a Thursday afternoon just after I got home from school. He looked to me like an overgrown teddy bear with his wild uncombed fuzzy grey hair and his plump appearance. He dressed always in a black leather coat with black trousers. I didn't realise it at the time, but I don't suppose he earned much money doing that job. Perhaps that's why he didn't have a wide variety of clothes to choose from in his wardrobe. He and I used to meet weekly.

We would always sit in the large sitting room of my parents' house, with me on the dark chocolate brown sofa and Matthew on a large matching chair at the other side of the room with a huge gilded coffee table between us, both

6

physically and emotionally a long way from where I was. We made idle chit-chat about this and that – I guess what grown-ups would call talking about the weather. The security he offered, by always showing up weekly at the same time, exerted a calming influence over me for a while, but still my behaviour deteriorated. Matthew probably knew a lot more about what was going on at home than he ever revealed to me. I was the one who was meant to guide the conversation, to talk about whatever was on my mind that week. Although in all honesty, the topic of conversation was so arbitrary that it probably only ever centred on what had happened that day at school. I rarely talked about my parents, mainly because there was nothing to say and nothing that could be said.

I was never into drugs like the two older girls in here. The only thing I ever did to break the law was to steal books from the school library. They never even found out. It was dead easy – I would select the books I wanted to steal and carry them into the putrid-smelling toilets nearby. I would sit myself down and then methodically search through every single page until I found the metal strip which, if left inside the book, would set the detector off as you walked through the library gates. With great pleasure and satisfaction, which made me tremble, I would rip out the metal strip, flush it away and then confidently walk out of the library after exchanging pleasantries with the middle-aged halfwit librarians. They all knew me in there and they all liked me too. That was the only hard bit about doing this stuff, that I knew they liked me and that they trusted me, because they were always nice to me. They smiled at me and made me feel that I was important, that I was noticed. But they sure weren't noticing those books going missing. Although when I got home I always panicked like mad. Every time the doorbell went or the phone rang I immediately thought that it was the police who had inevitably come to question me, if not to take me away. I had visions of ending up in prison for the rest of my childhood.

Although this is an adolescent unit for emotionally disturbed children, it's not dissimilar to a prison. It's called Redfield. The school that we all have to attend is just over the way, right opposite this building that we live in. The school is called Sea House but it isn't really like a school at all. There's lots of art and cooking and creative classes to attend, but they're a bit short on the academic side. Apparently most of the children who have been here are not overly academic anyway. They make us all do IQ tests when we first arrive and I remember that Miss Boyd told me that I had scored the highest ever – and that it was a very high IQ indeed. I urgently need a French teacher but there isn't one available so my French is completely going to pieces. I was even thinking of taking it up at A Level if I could get a good grade in it, but that isn't so likely now. Elaine is really good at maths – better than the teacher is, in fact, so she won't come on in any leaps and bounds either.

Aside from the serious lack of academic focus there are no music lessons provided here either, so I am unable to continue with my piano lessons – yet another punishment; a withdrawn privilege.

Apart from Elaine there is Rebecca aged seventeen and Siobhan aged sixteen and a half. Elaine and I are both the same age – nearly fourteen – so we hang around together most of the time. Although, don't misunderstand me, there is a real team spirit here amongst the girls, so to speak – more like a family than anything else. We've only got each other and we are more than aware of that. There are just the four of us girls admitted to Redfield at the moment, but there can be up to six at any given time. That's the maximum number, though. I guess that emotionally disturbed children are a bit much to handle so they keep the numbers low in order to control us all better. Too many of us wayward girls all in the same place and the nurses might have a riot on their hands! All in here for crimes against humanity! Well, for being emotionally disturbed, actually.

Primarily at some point prior to our admission to this place we each tried to kill ourselves. That seems to be the defining criterion for being sent to a place like this. Although in my case I attempted the annihilation thing at least a dozen times and then got expelled from school for cutting my wrists and dripping blood all over their highly polished floors. That and insulting the headmaster by phoning him at home and accusing him of being a liar and a hypocrite. He kind of brought it upon himself, though. He it was who had taught us in a philosophy class that the whole point of existence is to care – to care for others, ourselves, our world and so on. That care ought to constitute our very being itself. Well, when I then saw him shouting at a girl outside a classroom in the most uncaring manner one can imagine, I took it upon myself to call him at his home later that evening and to tell him what I thought of his caring character. That's how I ended up being called to his office the following day, when I was officially expelled.

After lunch was over, Elaine and I decided to head back into the school together. We both had art class with Sebastian. He is an inoffensive little man with short greyish white hair and an elf-like face. But he is completely boring and fake, like everyone else round here. He wears his home-made knitted jerseys daily, even in this boiling hot weather – and he never forgets to play his Bob Dylan tapes to us hour after endless hour. That man really knows how to make a feature of one's hurt! Elaine didn't say much to me on the way over. We enjoyed the brief walk out into the brilliant sunshine. She never speaks much anyway, but I like her regardless. She listens and you can tell that she is thinking about what you're saying, probably even trying to make sense of it, which is more than I could say for half the nurses looking out for us.

Elaine and I resumed our seats at the long white benches in the multicoloured paint-filled room and stuck pieces of shiny paper onto more shiny paper. This is supposed to demonstrate our ability to function as sane individuals in society!

'When I get out of here,' I quietly informed Elaine, 'I'll never go back to playschool again!' She smiled knowingly.

Rebecca and Siobhan were in pottery class so we had the benefit of Sebastian's expertise all to ourselves. That's the way they structure classes, so that we get individual attention and all that kind of thing. It's not a bad idea really, especially if a child is struggling in school and all that, as that kind of help can be just what they need – it builds confidence more than anything. Well, I think so, anyway. If they fail, then they know beforehand that the teacher isn't going to jump on them and put them down so that must help in itself. But as for me, I don't need it – I've always been top of my class and pretty much a straight A student. I even won an award for 'Student of the Year' – then they expelled me. There is irony in that. Somewhere.

I'm really only in Redfield for emotional disturbances – for being badly behaved – whereas some children can be admitted here just to attend the school. They are the lucky ones as they get to go home at the end of the day. I get to go upstairs to the 'cell' and be locked in all night, with one male nurse and one female nurse on duty all night. I don't sleep much either, certainly not well. Nightmares are a problem but I try to avoid that by keeping my eyes open for as long as I can manage it.

I kind of get through the night because Elaine wets the bed. She really won't like me telling you this stuff, but I figure that it can be just between us, right? Anyway, it happens at least three times a night – no kidding, she really does – and one rule they have in Redfield (amongst many) is that if you wet the bed then you have to change your own sheets, even in the middle of the night and all. There's a linen basket for dirty laundry at the end of the short corridor that has the washroom on the left and our 'cells' on the right. There's no way of escape as the door at the end of the corridor is locked every night as soon as we are sent up to bed at 9 p.m. There is a cupboard next to the bathroom with fresh sheets stored inside, which you can help yourself to at any time. So what happens is, Elaine always comes to me when she's had another 'accident' because the last thing that she's going to want to do is to tell the halfwit nurses that she's wet the bed like some two-year-old who can't control her bladder yet.

It's happened so many times that it is unspoken now – as soon as she appears hovering by my bedside I know what to do. I climb willingly out of bed and walk to her 'cell' and together we remove the urine-soaked sheets. The fresh and pungent smell does sometimes make me feel as though I'm going to be sick right there and then, but then I figure, at least I don't have to be in bed whiling away the long hours of the night with nothing else to do but fight off the demons inside me. Often a nurse will walk past and check to see what we're doing, but usually they just leave us to it – as long as I go straight back to bed after changing Elaine's sheets, the nurses are fairly cool. Elaine never says why she wets the bed, I don't think she knows. She is even woken up regularly throughout the night by a buzzer that they have placed beside her bed that goes off at short intervals. This is meant to wake her in time to go to the lavatory so that she doesn't have an accident, but it always seems to go off too late.

We never discuss the night's mishaps during the day; that's one thing I've learnt fast since being in Redfield. Whatever happened, happened – but it is never addressed or brought up unless the other person wants to. The nurses inform each one of us on the day of our admission here that we have to respect the fact that we each have our own problems and we are not to interfere with anyone else's behaviour or private life. Which is fair enough. I know that if it were me wetting the bed like that every night I absolutely wouldn't want anyone to remind me about it the next day over breakfast. It wouldn't sit well with my Cornflakes, that's a fact.

The next day my parents were coming here for their monthly visit. It was the first time since I'd been admitted to this crazy hospital that I would be allowed to see them. They have all these bizarre rules here and one of them is that you can't even speak to your parents on the telephone until you have been here for one month! The first month here was sheer agony. I had never really been away from home before.

Only when I was in hospital having open-heart surgery had I actually been away from home, but that's kind of different. For one thing I knew that needing heart surgery wasn't a punishment, whereas this sure as hell feels like a punishment. For the first week or two in here I think I cried nearly every day but the nurses were mainly unsympathetic to my plight. They would not allow me to call my parents – I was lucky if they even passed on a message to me from my parents saying that they had called to see how I was doing and all that.

Then the following month your parents, if they want to, are allowed to visit you on site so to speak – but only the once throughout an entire month. It's the weirdest set-up I've ever heard of, really. I kind of do want them to come and all that – I miss them terribly, like any child would be expected to under these circumstances – but at the same time I don't really want them to see me while I'm in here, locked up like this caged animal that is too dangerous to be let loose upon society. It really scares me that I'll never be allowed out and let back home again. I miss the strangest insignificant things, like my bedroom with its pink satin curtains with the frills and the tie-backs, and the freedom to do whatever I liked when I got home from school, at least until dinner time when my father would return home from work.

I miss playing around with my younger sister Kara who is eleven and my little baby brother Anthony. Anthony is the cutest baby you could ever see or even imagine. Anthony is two and a half now and he looks like a real little angel with his dark little curls falling all over his cherubic little face. He's the baby of the family and I'm the eldest, but I always feel closest to Anthony – maybe because he is as confused about this world as I am. He's learning what I am afraid that I will never be able to learn. I watch him closely as he is taught to walk and to eat by himself and to speak. I wonder how he feels and what he thinks, and if he has an inkling of the fact that he even exists. That is something that I am too painfully aware of. Existence truly is the bane of my life. I once told my mother this and she reacted with such confusion and annoyance that I have never seen since, either from her or on the face of anyone else.

As a small child I used to sit upon my mother's lap for ages, just playing with her – in my tiny little hands I would grip her jumper or her necklace or her finger. I would hold on so tight that I would convince myself that I would never have to let go if only she doesn't move. As long as she stays right here with me then I'll never want for anything. But she always moved. Inevitably I would be put down at some point and told to play by myself or go to sleep, or whatever other reason there was for leaving me. In my mind I felt the pain of the rejection as I experienced the feelings of abandonment that were occasioned by painful separations from my mother. The one person I truly loved and adored could so easily and suddenly let me go – even willingly push me away from her.

But now, being in Redfield, I am separated again from my mother and father. Although I miss them, it isn't unbearable. I kind of only miss Mummy, anyway. Daddy's too busy out at work most of the time to get to know too well. But I don't want to go into all that. He's a Councillor, so he's really busy. Everyone really loves my father – they all say how great he is and how hard he works 'for the community', which admittedly is a poor one. We don't live in some hotshot area you know, just an ordinary little town. Daddy's always trying to improve local services and all that sort of thing – he really cares about the community, does Daddy. That's probably why he's been re-elected three times to hold the same seat in the Council for three years running. All the people love him, and really, there's no reason not to.

It's Mummy that I worry about the most. She is kind of dependent on Daddy for everything – the house, food, clothes, everything. You name it and Mummy relies on Daddy to provide it. I know she really loves him, though. That's probably why she doesn't see anything but good in him.

'Oh, hi, Elaine … I'm just coming … gimme a sec.' Yawning, I clambered out of bed and felt around on the soft carpet floor for my pink piggy slippers. They were a present from my grandparents who thought that I would like them because they are pink. Pink is my favourite colour and at home my bedroom is decorated entirely in pink. It's so pink that my Mother often jokes about the fact that she needs to wear shades in order to be able to see anything in my room!

I went in to help Elaine change her sheets for the second time that evening. Surprisingly, I was actually asleep when she appeared standing beside my bed. She had gently placed her hand upon me, knowing that that would be more than enough to wake me. My dream had just started to take a downturn into the dark avenues of demons and night terrors that so often beset me when I dare to fall into that unprotected region of sleep. Hence I gladly welcomed the awakening by Elaine. We went into her cell and I sleepily helped her to change her soaking wet bed sheets. I stripped Elaine's bed while she brought fresh sheets from the linen cupboard with which to replace the old ones. We did all this in our usual ritual of silence, partly from fear of disturbing the nurses as well as the other two girls who were asleep in their respective 'cells'.

14

Yet I don't actually have a 'cell' of my own. I prefer to remain in the main dorm area, which is used for new admissions. There are three beds in here and the light from the nurses' office is visible throughout the whole night. If you have trouble sleeping you can even hear the soft murmur of their voices as they talk in hushed tones to each other. I don't know why, but it's a fact that I just feel safer in here. In a room of my own I would feel more vulnerable. Not that I told the nurses that. I just asked not to be moved into a room of my own after my trial period was through. This usually lasts for the first few weeks of admission. If you behave yourself then you are 'rewarded' by being allowed a private bedroom along the corridor. But I'm staying put, so if any new girls arrive they will share with me, but for the moment I am alone.

The 'dorm' space itself is much larger than a single bedroom 'cell' is anyway. It's a lot less private though, as the nurses just walk through it at all hours to do those nightly checks on us girls. I always pretend to be asleep but my heart pounds so fast inside me that I often fear that the nurse will hear it as he or she walks past my bed. There are small windows above the beds on each side of the wall but they open just a fraction, and would be impossible to climb out of.

There is also an imitation pine wardrobe beside each bed, but I don't know why they bother giving us wardrobes for 'privacy' to hang up our clothes. As soon as you arrive at Redfield and have undergone the very intrusive medical examination, a psychiatric nurse is allocated to you. She then systematically goes through your suitcase with you as you unpack and withholds anything from you that is deemed to be dangerous.

The nurse Harriet who checked my suitcase with me has hardly had a civil word out of me since that first day of my arrival. I can barely look her in the face, let alone speak to her. Harriet was all very pleasant about it and cheery – even apologetic – but it felt so invasive, having my belongings

15

gone through like that. There was nothing left for me. Nothing of my own that even felt like mine any more. Even my teddy bear felt like a stranger, until that first night in bed anyway when I held on to Pooh Bear so tight that I'm surprised I didn't break him. I was 'institutionalised' and there wasn't a damn thing in the world that I could do about it.

Chapter 2

'Wakey wakey, rise and shine.' And so began my morning. Bryony woke me from a light slumber as she came breezing through the dorm and then calling out in her high-pitched voice, as she leant across my immobile form beneath the sheets to open up the faded tattered orange curtains hanging limply above my bed. These particular curtains had holes in them where they were so badly frayed at the edges. Often at night I would lie awake wondering why nobody had noticed these holes and changed the curtains, or mended them at least.

Bryony is fairly large for her small height but homely looking. Like a mum, really, but I don't think I would ever tell her that. I mean, what do mums look like anyway? I don't suppose there are any hard and fast rules about those sorts of things. Anyone can have a child, but not anyone can have a dog. At least not without some sort of background check or reference. I never could work that one out. Bryony's hair is blonde and wavy with tight little ringlets at the nape of her neck, which always look as though they are trying to escape from her otherwise tightly pinned up hair. Matronly and efficient, she always made sure that us girls were up in time for breakfast, even showered and dressed before we made it to the breakfast table.

That's another strict rule at this place, no pyjamas to be worn at the dining table. Not unless you are on punishment

17

that is – then pyjamas are all that you are allowed to wear. No kidding, they even send you off to school in your pyjamas if you're on punishment. If you've done something wrong then the whole damn world is going to know about it. So far, I haven't been on punishment and that sure is a surprise, considering my behaviour at home and at my previous school. Imagine that – having to attend school in the outside world in your pyjamas if you've been naughty!

I guess I'd misbehave just to be able to get out of wearing that awful grey school uniform that I was forced to wear at Harrington High School for Girls. The skirt had pleats at the front and it really was the most unflattering article of clothing I have ever had to wear in my entire life. Well, that and those white hospital gowns that don't do up at the back and so they always expose your bottom to the whole ward when it's your turn to climb onto the trolley which takes you into the operating theatre. Those porters must see more bottoms in their whole life than anyone else. Probably even more than doctors, because at least doctors get to see other parts of the body as well. But those hospital porters, really all they do the whole day long is carry virtually naked people to operating theatres and back again.

At breakfast Elaine and I ate our Cornflakes pretty much in silence. We had both been up most of the night, and no doubt the day nurses had read the reports that the night nurses had left behind. All these nurses, they always know what's going on even if they don't let on that they know. You can bet your life that they know every last word you even spoke before you went to bed. The reason I know this is because I see them scribbling away at their reports at the end of each shift.

It was a Saturday and the day that my parents were meant to be visiting. To pass the time I asked Elaine to play pool with me, which she did, after the nurses handed over the cues. We were in the middle of our second game when I looked up and there they were standing right before me, as though they had never even left me here in the first place. They looked kind of awkward and out of place. Mummy especially looked nervous. Daddy stood there and smiled a beaming great big grin at me, almost as though he'd just won the pool game and not me. Fear gripped hold of me and for a few seconds left me frozen and speechless. Elaine quietly sneaked away so that I didn't even notice her absence until I turned to introduce her and found that she wasn't there beside the pool table. The charge nurse Bryony offered my parents a cup of tea and they politely accepted. Probably they were worried that if they refused her offer of tea then the nurses would think that they were mad too, and lock them up for all eternity.

We sat down on the faded orange chairs and I pulled mine round to face my parents, otherwise we would have all been lined up against the wall like soldiers in a firing line. The conversation turned to the drive up here, the weather and the health and happiness of my two siblings all in a space of ten minutes. By the time Bryony returned with the tea there didn't seem like much else was left to say. Mummy looked as though she wanted to know more, to ask me some questions, perhaps, but Daddy steered all conversation away from my current predicament. It was almost as though I weren't even in this place, locked up, trapped and stripped of all rights and freedom. They just wanted to carry on as normal as though we were at home having some pleasant little tea party. Only this didn't feel much like a tea party from where I was sitting.

Mummy looked pretty in her Laura Ashley light blue print dress with her light brown hair falling just past her shoulders and delicately curling just underneath. Mummy is petite, like me in fact. I have very long light brown hair with masses of unruly ringlets; it falls right down to my waist, but so did my mother's hair when she was my age. I'm a bit heavier than

Mummy though, and it shows. She weighs far too little for her height really, because she hardly ever eats and she swims nearly every morning. Daddy looked as important and business-like as ever, dressed as he was in one of his smart work suits. At home I have known him on some rare occasion to sit around in jeans and sweatshirts, but not when he is expecting visitors and definitely not when he leaves the house.

'First impressions count my girl,' he repeatedly tells me in the midst of his endless criticisms of my sloppy style of dress, and my perpetual inability to care about my clothes or for that matter my appearance.

Daddy's hair is short, always neatly trimmed and a shade darker than mine and Mummy's. Only Kara's hair is the same as Daddy's in terms of its colouring. Daddy wears glasses when he reads – round gold framed owl-type glasses, they make him look really intellectual and he gets teased about this a lot from us children. He doesn't seem to mind though. Sometimes Daddy's OK, you know. He will let you joke around and have a laugh with him about all sorts, even the way he looks and all, but at other times, well he just changes and he won't laugh any more. Even if you said the exact same thing that you were saying the day before, he won't laugh at it. He might even tell you to go to your room, to leave him in peace or something. No kidding, that's my father for you. Totally inconsistent.

Kara always seems to make him smile though, no matter what mood he is in when he gets home from work. Daddy will sit down in his armchair in the corner, the big one that Matthew Richards used to sit on when he visited me weekly, and he kicks off his shoes and just leaves them right there where they land. At this point Kara always runs to fetch Daddy's slippers for him from the cloakroom that we have built in underneath our staircase.

Kara's only eleven and the prettiest child around. In the

class photo that she brought home just before I was admitted to Redfield you can see that she stands out more than any other child. She has the same beaming smile that Daddy has. Her hair is even longer than mine – almost reaching her bottom in fact. She's a graceful child, what with the way she moves and everything. Mummy pays for her to attend ballet classes so she's learned how to move and hold herself properly when she walks. I'm never allowed to do that stuff on the grounds that I have a weak heart; it might just quit working if I strain it too much, that's what the doctors tell me anyway. Mummy always takes their word on everything because they are meant to be experts and all that.

I argue with the doctors all the time about these ridiculous limits that they set for my activities, but no one really listens to me even though it's my heart, in my body. I once told Dr Miller that I'd rather be allowed to do the same things that children my own age do and die young, knowing that I have lived, rather than live the way they tell me but never really doing anything more than any geriatric person does. They just put that reasoning down to my strong suicidal tendencies and ignored me.

After their cups of tea were finished Mummy said that they really ought to be getting back home now, as Anthony and Kara would be missing them. 'They are really too young to understand what this place is for and why you're here so we couldn't bring them,' Mummy explained. 'You understand don't you? Why we couldn't expose them to this, I mean ...' she explained, guilt appearing all over her face.

The truth was that Daddy had probably decided that bringing my brother and sister along for a family visit would only serve to reward me for my expulsion from school. As for the countless suicide attempts prior to my admission to Redfield, they were not even acknowledged. Ever.

'You take care,' Mummy said to me as we reached the door. Bryony was chaperoning us – no doubt so that I wouldn't escape – but that was highly unlikely. My parents weren't likely to aid in setting me free. 'We really want you to get well, that's all,' explained Mummy as she said goodbye, leaving me there, alone again. Daddy smiled his beaming grin in my direction and made some witty remark about the water supplies drying up this way as I reluctantly let a tear escape and trickle down my cheek.

I headed for concealment by returning to the 'ward'. More than anything I wanted privacy just then, to be able to go and hide in my bed with Pooh Bear, up in the dorm, maybe even cry my heart out at the loss of my mother. But that was forbidden. I just about made it to the toilet before Charlotte, another less senior nurse on duty, asked me if I was feeling OK.

'Fine,' I snapped back at her. 'I just want to go to the toilet … is that still allowed?' I angrily stated as I stormed off into the nearest lavatory. As soon as I was behind that locked door I virtually collapsed onto the cold stone floor and let the tears stream down my face. They were unstoppable; I so much wanted to get out of here. I yearned for my freedom with my whole being, as I shook with the force of each sob. Thoughts of Kara and Anthony were racing through my mind. I tried to conjure up pictures of them but couldn't seem to hold their image for any length of time. I was afraid that I would never see them again.

It wasn't long before Charlotte returned with the key to the toilet. 'If you don't come out, Lucy, I'll have to unlock the door. I do have the key, I must warn you.'

I instantly opened the door, more out of a sense of pride than anything else. I didn't want some nurse to beat me, to think that I was vulnerable and needed rescuing from some lousy toilet. Charlotte looked at me sympathetically, I suppose, but I just shrugged past her and made my way back into the recreation area. I flung myself into a chair and pretended to flick through the nearest glossy magazine that I could lay my hands on. It was probably a donated back copy of *Sugar* or *Just Seventeen* or something else as inane as that. I wasn't really reading it so much as using it to hide behind. Elaine didn't approach me at this point. It was clear to her that I wanted to be left alone, so why wasn't it clear to the halfwit nurses, I asked myself in frustration. I forced myself to concentrate on some article about the lack of vitamin E in our diets and how it is extremely important for healthy skin. I started to panic that I wasn't getting enough vitamin E and asked Charlotte if she would get some tablets for me the next time that she went into town. I asked her to bring them in on her next shift, which would be in a few days' time.

All the nurses worked a short rota here, so that it would only be a matter of days before we saw the same nurses on duty again. This was meant to encourage us to build up relationships with them and get to know them. I'm telling you, it's like an artificial family in this place, it really is. Charlotte said that she would see what she could do, but I kind of knew that she would forget or just not bother. What do they care if I have to walk around looking like a decomposing corpse? It's not their problem.

The day passed relatively slowly and Sunday was pretty much the same, except for the fact that on Sundays we were all taken across to the gym after our evening meal, and allowed to play badminton against each other and the nurses. In my case permission had to be sought from the cardiologist at the specialist heart hospital I attend in London before I was allowed to set foot on the badminton court. That's one of the problems with having a serious heart condition. Everyone around you expects you to just drop dead at any moment. But really, in my case, there's no such luck.

It was fun playing badminton, especially as it was a new experience. I had never been allowed to play before as it had always been considered too much of a risk for me to participate in games or physical education at school. But this was only light-hearted fun, the games were not serious, and they were not overly demanding. Also I was expected to stop and rest as soon as I felt tired or breathless. If I failed to do this then a nurse would invariably tap me on the shoulder and suggest that I take a break, even if it meant interfering with the game. Yet I complied immediately out of fear of being forbidden to play any more if I refused to take a rest when ordered.

A nurse would usually take over my position in the game when this happened. Invariably Elaine and I paired up against Siobhan and Rebecca. Rebecca is a lot shorter than Siobhan's towering five foot eleven inches and so it evened out pretty fairly, as I am a lot smaller than Elaine who equally towers over me. Rebecca's lovely straight long blonde hair was always flowing behind her as she ran to hit the shuttlecock, and I often thought how much like a fairytale princess she looked. I think she knows it, though, if the amount of time that she spends in front of the mirror in the bathroom is anything to judge by! Although my hair is longer than Rebecca's, it is not blonde and so it doesn't quite have the same impact as her golden locks.

I love the woody smell of the gym, the wooden shiny polished floors, the benches, and the net across the badminton court. It really was a whole new world to me, one that I was never allowed to enter before I was admitted here. Always being excluded on the grounds of my congenital heart condition, I never expected to be allowed to do this until I was eighteen when I would start making my own rules about how strenuous a life I wanted to lead. When resting I soaked up the atmosphere of the gym and watched the others running to hit the shuttlecock before it lands on the floor and I sometimes managed to forget even where I was and what I was doing here. I often looked at the ropy netting which is used for climbing and wondered what it would feel like to climb that, to make it to the top and feel that sense of freedom and achievement.

'Right girls, it's time to head back now – it's nearly 8 p.m. You can have some supper and then it's time for bed, so finish off your game soon or continue it next time,' said Adam loudly in order to grab everyone's attention. He was fairly cool and would often let us go to bed a little bit past 9 p.m. providing we were all behaving ourselves. He was the senior nurse in charge this evening so the other nurse also on duty did not dare to argue with him. He was too pleasant to disagree with, anyway.

Sweating and hot we collected together our rackets and jumpers and left the gym. First we changed from our plimsolls into our outdoor shoes. We all wore trainers but mine have these lights at the back, which flash when I walk, and boy am I teased about this.

'Traffic lights,' I heard Siobhan call out from behind me.

'Ha ha,' I replied and turned to face her. With her dark skin and tall slim figure she looked down on me from her five feet eleven inches, as opposed to my four feet eleven and a half inches. Against the dark night I could just about make out that she smiled and so I smiled back. No harm was intended. The older girls felt that it was their duty to tease us younger ones out of some sort of artificial filial duty, no doubt.

I was relieved to get into the shower as soon as we got back from the gym. I declined the tempting offer of hot chocolate with toast so that I could spend longer in the shower scrubbing away at my dirty infected skin. If I could have my way I would shower at least six times a day. Getting myself clean is too difficult a task to achieve, I guess, and that applies to inside and out. The hot soothing water bursting from the showerhead onto my soft skin was and always is a welcome relief. The soapy bubbles amidst the steam engulfing my fragile body offers momentary release for my otherwise heavily laden guilt-ridden self.

I remained in the shower until Rebecca started banging on the door for her turn. I yelled out that I wouldn't be much longer and quickly towel-dried my dripping wet body and put my nightdress on while I was still half wet. This meant that my nightdress clung to my skin but I didn't much care. I managed to blow-dry my long hair and then I climbed into my uninviting bed and was tucked up with Pooh Bear before nine, although I was, as usual, apprehensive about the night ahead. Adam was on nights, so that wasn't too bad. I felt the most safe with him around, even though he is a man. He's kind of not a man at the same time. He reminds me of my mother in lots of ways that I couldn't even name to myself let alone begin to describe to you. You'll just have to take my word for it, although no one else takes my word for anything so I see no reason why you would anyway.

The lights in the dorm were switched off and I heard Adam call to the girls along the corridor to turn their own bedroom lights out. He stood there for a moment to see that his instructions were followed, which of course they were. I noticed the lighting in the dorm get distinctly dimmer as the lights along the corridor were extinguished. The 'cells' each have heavyset doors with tiny windows built into them which means that any light automatically shines through. It also means that any nurse can walk by and see what the girls are doing at any given moment – even getting changed and all that, which is really weird, if you ask me. I held my breath as he walked past my bed and through the dorm into the nurses' office. He said, 'Goodnight, Lucy,' as he passed by, and I replied softly without really wanting to draw his attention to myself in any way. I just wanted him to go away, away from my bed and far away from me. Which he did.

'No … No … No … I'm sorry … please no … please … I'm sorry … I'll be a good girl … please no …' at which point I woke up, sweat mingled with tears pouring down my face, the thin bedcovers kicked off onto the floor where they were in a jumbled heap of their own, with Adam standing beside them, looking at me. He was trying to place himself in my line of vision so that I wouldn't be taken by surprise at his unexpected presence.

'What do you want?' I half sobbed out.

'I came to see if you're all right, I don't like to hear anyone crying. I wondered if you'd like to talk?' Adam spoke soothingly and began to gather up my bedclothes in his arms.

At this point I became aware of the soaking wet sheet beneath me. For the first time in my life I had wet the bed. Adam had noticed this fact also by this time – from the feel of the crumpled sheets that he picked up from the floor no doubt. He told me not to worry because it could happen to anyone, then he went away saying that he'd be back in a moment with fresh sheets. I drew my knees up to my chin and sobbed. Pooh Bear seemed to be lost, he certainly wasn't on my bed any longer, and I felt the loneliness of my existence without the only friend I have in the world.

Adam returned and suggested that I take a shower and change into a fresh nightdress.

'Am I going to be on punishment for this?' I asked tentatively, not really knowing why I felt as though I were going to be punished.

'No, of course not, there is no reason for you to be punished. You really haven't done anything wrong.' Somehow I felt that there was more being said behind Adam's words, that he was speaking these words to some other part of me that desperately needed to hear this.

I took myself off into the shower, but not before Elaine had put her head outside her bedroom door and enquired if I was OK. 'Yeah, sure, I'm fine' I replied, still stifling sobs. Once inside the shower cubicle I stripped as fast as I could. The water from the shower was hot at first but I really didn't care – the hotter the water and the more scorching it was the better it would be to cleanse me. I scrubbed and scrubbed away at my dirty defiled skin and thought that if only I could take vitamin E tablets then I might at least have a chance of making myself better if not cleaner. I knew there and then that I had to get out of this place, to be able to have my life back again, make choices of my own.

Once dried and dressed in a clean nightdress I went back to my dorm. Adam was sitting there on my freshly made-up bed holding Pooh Bear gently in his arms. He rose up to let me get past him and into bed when he saw me approaching. He passed my faithful bear to me, who thankfully was all dry. Once in bed Adam asked if he could fetch me a drink or anything. I declined this offer and thanked him for making up my bed.

'It's a pleasure, Lucy, really. If you need anything then call me, OK? If you want to talk about ... stuff ... then just let me know, that's what I'm here for.'

He hesitated when he said 'stuff' as though I ought to know what he meant by that. These psychiatric nurses, they think they know you so damn well just because you have one lousy nightmare and wet the bed for once in your life.

I had quit crying by now, and snuggled down with my bear determined not to fall into the trap of going to sleep again. I vowed there and then never to sleep again, but somehow even I knew that sleep would eventually overtake me. I fought sleep with all my might every single night, and resented being sent off to bed to have to face this torturous journey through the dark hours. But for the rest of that night I lay awake, thinking of how when I grew up I would be famous and all – maybe an actress or some hotshot film producer, something like that. I imagined what it would be like to have been Marilyn Monroe or Madonna, to be anyone else but myself. What would it be like to live someone else's life and have all the vitamin E that you need and whenever you want it too, so that you don't have to put up with unhealthy looking skin.

I reasoned that if you were an actress then you would have to summon up all your energy to be able to get so into that role that it must be at least possible to forget who you really are. If you can forget who you are then all the horrible stuff inside that goes round with you will have to go away too. What would it be like to play Ophelia, I wondered, to drown myself all for the love of a man who was prepared to pack me off to a convent? So Hamlet didn't want me – well, I wouldn't kill myself over that. I never could understand how Ophelia could do that. That's no reason worthy of suicide.

To die is to honour life, and to die by your own hand is to pronounce something in life worth dying for. Well, Ophelia got it wrong, as far as I'm concerned. No man is worth dying for. If I were to kill myself it would have to be over something really important, like the failure to find out who I really am for one thing. Or the failure to find any meaning in this life. Really important stuff such as that. The rest of the night dragged on in this manner, with occasional checks by Adam. I pretended to be asleep when he passed by through the dorm, but I regretted the fake snoring that I had put on on one occasion when I sensed his footsteps approaching, in case it had been too obvious that I was only pretending to be unconscious. Adam didn't comment either way, but then he wouldn't, would he.

He did however hesitate beside my bed for a few moments. I immediately sensed his presence and stopped snoring in order to hold my breath. If I pretend I am not here then he might go away … but Daddy never did go away because he always knew that I was there after all, just pretending not to exist so that he wouldn't come near me or be able to find me. Adam did return back to the nurses' office after a few terrifying moments. Eventually the pounding of my heart slowed down to a more reasonable rate.

The dim light from the nurses' office cast a warm low light throughout the dorm where I was meant to be sleeping. I felt safe here even with a male nurse just minutes away from where I slept. For reasons I couldn't fathom, Adam didn't frighten me as much as other men. Or at least not as much as Daddy frightened me.

Elaine didn't disturb me throughout the rest of the night either, even though I was hoping that she would. I wanted something to do, to keep me awake by force if my effort were to fail me. Elaine's bed-wetting would have been a welcome distraction, although I seemed to have done that job by myself tonight. Why did that happen? How could that happen ... to me? I don't wet the bed. But I couldn't deny the fact that I just had. At least I was not in any trouble. Imagine if that had happened at home. My father would have virtually killed me, I'm sure of it. Wetting the bed at the age of thirteen would have been totally unacceptable. Even to my own mind it is, but I knew that I damn well didn't intend to do it. Just saying no to my father when he makes me do stuff that I don't like always results in a severe punishment, so bed-wetting would probably have meant death. Even Mummy would have been angry about having to clean the bed sheets. But here in Redfield they don't make you feel responsible for anything at all like this. The nurses here are cool in that way, accepting that accidents are just accidents and all that sort of thing. I haven't been punished for anything since I got here. Not even for crying at night-time when I feel scared after a bad dream.

However, I must have fallen into another deep yet undisturbed sleep later that same night because the next thing that I remember was the sun streaming into the dorm and Bryony standing over me waking me up in time for breakfast.

Chapter 3

Charlotte, who was the junior nurse on duty that day, walked across with me to Jarvis House. All children are supposed to be escorted into this building. Probably so we don't run off or set fire to the building or something like that. Seriously, Siobhan – she set fire to her old school once when she was about ten! She told me that it gave her the biggest buzz of her life. But that's not why she's locked up in here; well, it's not the only reason. Arson's not for me though. I wouldn't want to do that, mainly because I'm dead scared of fire and also in case I killed some innocent person who was inside the building at the time. Imagine going up in flames like that, being scorched by a thousand flames licking at your defence-less body. Scares the hell out of me just thinking about it.

Jarvis House is right next to the school building but separate enough from it not to be part of the school. My weekly appointment with Mr Williams is at 11 a.m. I was actually allowed to miss school classes for this therapy, so I kind of liked it for that reason alone. School's not so challenging here, you know. After walking slowly along the shiny polished wooden floor with office doors on either side of the white-walled corridor, we reached Mr Williams's consulting room. Charlotte left me outside sitting on one of the brown hardback chairs, right next to a big green leafy plant.

The door was slightly ajar so Mr Williams knew that I had

arrived. At exactly 11 a.m. Mr Williams stepped outside of his office and stood in front of his creaky wooden door. He asked in the same kind soft voice that he always addressed me with 'Would you like to step inside Lucy?' Without answering him I just walked right past him and sat myself down in the big soft pale pink armchair that was always placed just underneath the only window in the room.

By sitting here I could see the door the whole time. That's important to me. I remember that I told Mr Williams about this little idiosyncrasy of mine at our first meeting – just to ensure that he always kept that chair free for me, you know, without trying to sit in it himself before I could get there, so to speak. But he started to analyse me right there and then. Well, he tried to anyhow, but I just told him bluntly that I didn't want to hear about being trapped in my mother's womb and all that drivel. Not that he offered that by way of analysis, I just didn't want to discuss this preference of mine. I mean, it's just a door, right. What's so significant about that anyway?

We began therapy pretty much in silence. He tried to engage me in a conversation by politely enquiring how I felt. 'OK,' was my sharp reply.

Looking at him, I would have to say that Mr Williams is not an unattractive man. He actually looks quite becoming. He dresses really well for a man his age – I mean, he's about forty and all. I know this for a fact because I asked him once how old he was. Probably in our first therapy session together – I am cheeky like that. After telling me in no uncertain terms that we are here to discuss me, he reluctantly admitted to being 'around forty'. Usually he wears jeans or chinos and a really cool shirt. Quite plain colours like blue and brown and beige and that sort of thing, but he dresses with style. His hair is wavy and nearly shoulder length. It amazes me that he's allowed to keep his hair so long in a job like his; you'd think there'd be a rule that he would have to at least *look* responsible and *look* like a therapist.

'I hear you had a bad night last night. Would you like to discuss it?'

'Isn't there anything private in this lousy place?'

To this statement which I uttered pretty much in anger and with a sense of felt betrayal, Mr Williams informed me that he is given a weekly report on me which I am already aware of. 'But we don't have to discuss this if you don't want to. It might help though. After all, the fact that you had a nightmare like that might indicate that therapy is working.'

'Working! Working!' I spluttered out half in amazement and half in fury. 'How on earth can it be working when you know nothing about me and even less about my nightmares!' I demanded to know.

'I understand you are upset and even angry with me. But I am here to help you Lucy. If you would just tell me about your dream then we could start fighting this thing, you know.' He looked at me as though I ought to know what 'thing' he was referring to. I guessed I did know somewhere deep inside me. But boy, I'd rather not go there if I could help it.

I sat there in stony silence, listening to the ticking of the clock as the minute hand continued uninterrupted and unaffected by the emotionally charged atmosphere in this small consulting room. I'm sure glad there are plenty of plants in here, because at times like this I feel as though I'm going to stop breathing. At least the plants will keep me going with their discarded oxygen.

'So what are you going to say now? ... Tell me about your childhood?' I taunted, but to no avail.

Mr Williams smiled kindly and asked even more earnestly, 'Would you like to tell me about your childhood, Lucy? We could start there ... if you're happy to?' His eyes bore into my soul with a gaze that was completely fixed on me. As though whatever I would say would be really important. He was waiting for my response, so I averted my eyes while I contemplated what to say to this man in order to show him once and for all who was in charge. Nothing came to mind apart from graphic images of brutality.

It would be unthinkable to share those thoughts with someone as kind to me as Mr Williams so I said nothing. What would he think of me, if he knew … would he still care to listen so much then? I asked myself this question repeatedly about every halfwit person I ever met at Redfield. All these nurses, claiming that they just want to help and all that – 'If only you would talk to us, Lucy,' they keep telling me. But how can I talk when … when … jees, they don't realise … they just don't know … the danger I would be in for a start, and not just me. I could not talk, not about that.

Mr Williams was still looking intently at me when I dared to face him again. He really was a kind man, genuinely trying to 'help' me – whatever that means – I could see that in the lines and creases of his skin which are all across his face. No doubt this job had aged him considerably. Putting up with children like me can't be an easy choice. If I were a poncey therapist I wouldn't work here, no way. I'd go off and find work in some private practice in some hotshot area like London and I'd charge a hundred pounds for only one measly hour of my time. That's all you get when you're in therapy, you know – one hour a week, and that's supposed to 'cure' you! It's not even an hour though – it's always fifty minutes, 'the analytic hour' they call it! By the time you get around to saying anything really important it's always time to get up and leave anyhow. Not that I ever say anything really important to Mr Williams.

After some brief exchanges about the forthcoming ice-skating trip, Mr Williams called it a day. He reminded me to wear gloves and wrap up warm, as the ice is pretty cold, especially if you fall onto it.

The nurses were arranging a trip out for us to the local ice rink in Gillingham. I had never been there before so I didn't even know if I could ice-skate. But I was fairly good on roller blades so was hoping that it was not going to be vastly different. Rebecca had told me the previous night before bedtime that she had been ice-skating since the age of three, and she offered to teach me how to do it.

After therapy was over Charlotte was waiting outside of the consulting room for me. We walked back together in silence mostly. The nurses never asked about therapy appointments or anything. They tried to appear to respect your privacy and all, but I know they all keep writing stuff down about me every single day so they read it all there anyway. I guess they don't even need to ask me what I think about stuff, because they just ask each other if they want to know anything about me and all.

When I got back to Redfield it was time for lunch which we all ate rather hurriedly. School at Sea House always finished at 2 p.m. so we were all dressed and ready to go by 2.30 p.m. Charlotte drove the minibus round and stopped it right outside Redfield unit. We were all rather excited and clambered in the rusty white old bus as fast as we could. The nurses on duty were Charlotte, Harriet and Andy. They were taking me, Siobhan, Rebecca and Elaine to the ice-skating rink as a reward for good behaviour. We had 'proved' ourselves capable of being trusted – mainly because none of us has tried to escape or got up to any mischievous behaviour since we have been admitted to this unit.

As the minibus drove down the winding country lanes on its way out of the countryside and on to the motorway, the girls were all chattering excitedly in the back. I didn't say much or even listen to their conversation. My attention was caught by the outside world and I tried to imagine myself in the sky or in the trees, to lose myself just for a moment. It's something I learnt to do once, which kind of works if you need to forget where you are or what's happening, if only for a second. Not that I needed to forget where I was right then, but it's kind of a habit now anyway. I find myself doing it just because I can, because it's always safe.

When we pulled into the coach park, Andy, the senior charge nurse, turned to address us girls. 'You know the rules, girls. We stay together. When you've got your skates go straight on to the ice rink and skate around as much as you like. We want you to have fun, but be careful. Definitely don't push anyone over, and don't be a nuisance. Otherwise we will ask you to sit down and spend the remainder of the time just watching the others – OK? If you get any problems come to one of us. Do you get that, girls?' he asked loudly in case we had all gone suddenly deaf.

'Yeah!' we each yelled back.

The cold freshness of the ice hit me in the face as soon as we entered the ice rink. My entire body felt chilled and gripped by this awesome icy dome. The loud thumping pop music irritated me as it belted out the latest in chart music. People, young and old, were just racing round and round in this ice-filled circle, flashes of colour – reds and greens and purples and yellows – whizzed past as sweatshirts buzzed along keeping time to the music. Some of the skaters were even singing along. I tentatively ventured to put my first foot on the ice, having done up and redone up my boots for the third time.

'Make sure they're tight,' the lady handing out the skates over the counter told me. So I had to keep rechecking them to make sure that they were tight enough. When my boots were so tightly laced that I could barely feel the blood circulating in my legs, I stepped onto the ice. Rebecca wasn't too far behind my initially shaky start, ready to catch me or to push me forward if I needed her expert assistance.

Surprisingly I took to ice-skating like a duck to water. I felt the freedom of my body as I glided almost effortlessly through the air and round the circular dome. The rhythmic motion of skating and the mind-numbing music was a welcome relief from the therapy session this morning and a distraction from all unwelcome thoughts.

At half-time the nurse Andy called out to us. We went into the cafeteria and the nurses bought us a flat Coke and dry packet of crisps each. We were even allowed to keep our skates on, but it was not easy trying to walk across the tarmac in ice skates. I fell into Siobhan at least twice but she just told me to get lost and that was cool. After the short break we were allowed back onto the ice rink for one final hour. Then we were expected to leave the dome and meet in the foyer at the exit.

I must admit that thoughts of escaping did flash through my mind like an out of control roller-coaster. But thoughts of where I would actually be able to go or even how I would get there were few and far between. So I stayed with the others and climbed back into the minibus when it was time to head back to Redfield. The journey back was undertaken in a great deal of silence. Rebecca was a bit offish with me when I spoke to her, and I genuinely couldn't figure out why. The nurse Charlotte said something about Rebecca feeling a bit jealous that I could skate as well as her when I'd never done it before and all that. Jees, that's no reason to ditch your friends, right. It's not my fault that I can skate as well as she can. So that said, we all sulked and were silent until we pulled into the grounds of Redfield. It was pitch dark when we arrived back and bedtime wasn't far off.

The nurses on night duty were Adam and Bryony. While the day nurses handed over in the office we took it in turns to have a shower. Elaine was really exhausted and was asleep before I had even had a chance to say goodnight to her.

Rebecca pushed past me as I was leaving the bathroom so that I dropped my Pooh Bear wash bag. For this I pushed her right back. She started yelling at me, so without thinking about it I scratched the side of her face with my long nails. The noise attracted the attention of the nurses who came running to the bathroom to find out what was going on. They called both Rebecca and myself into the office. There was blood trickling down the side of Rebecca's face. Considering the facts, I could hardly deny scratching her. I did feel afraid about the possible punishment for this outburst but the nurses were dead cool about it. They asked Rebecca and I to apologise to each other and to make friends again. Which we did. I was very surprised – even Rebecca wanted to be my friend again. So we made up there and then and she never even minded about the scratch on her face or anything. It wasn't even mentioned again, in spite of the fact that the jagged red scratch mark remained there for several days.

That night I lay in bed for ages just thinking about the ice-skating trip – how pleasant it had been to feel the icy air, to glide around like a free bird without a care in the world. The music too loud to allow room even to think, let alone to feel anything but frozen. Maybe when I'm older I'll be a professional skater, then I could wear all those short frilly little dresses all the time and I would have the most perfect legs. Those girls, they always have perfect legs.

I drifted off to sleep thinking about myself in a frilly pink satin dress ice-skating with Torvill on my right and Dean on my left. Dean was saying how much he would rather swop Torvill for this new 'wonder girl'. Everyone in the auditorium was applauding as loudly as they could, while Dean was whirling me around really fast so that my head was spinning. The next thing I knew I was seated on the sofa in the living room at home. Daddy was standing, towering over me, telling me that I was in serious trouble this time. I was unable to lift my eyes from the thick black leather belt around his waist. The black leather had a slight tear that was barely visible next to the shiny metal buckle. As Daddy spoke I concentrated more and more on the tear on his leather belt, wondering why the torn leather looked white beneath the deep black surface.

'Are you listening to me, Lucy?' His angry question broke into my concentration and propelled me back with a jolt.

Facing him now, looking up at him and daring to meet his hard stare I answered timidly, 'Yes, Daddy.'

After a few minutes of anguished silence during which time Daddy just looked at me, as if deciding my fate there and then, he spoke again. In a stern but fairly quiet voice he ordered, 'Go up to your room, Lucy, remove your skirt and wait for me.'

Knowing what was going to happen I started to plead with him to spare me. 'Daddy please don't punish me, please believe me, Daddy, I'm so sorry. I won't do it again, please don't punish me ...' The desperate pleading words came tumbling out as Daddy was standing over me. Daddy ordered me once more to go my room but when I didn't move from the sofa he grabbed me with both hands. he forcibly grabbed hold of my arm and marched me out of the sitting room into the hallway and up the stairs.

On the way up the stairs I knocked my head against the staircase wall as I struggled to wriggle free from Daddy's vice-like grip. He didn't relent and continued to virtually pull me up the stairs with my feet barely even touching each step. There was no sound other than my futile protests and frantic pleading with him to let me go. When we reached the top of the stairs he opened my bedroom door with his free hand and pushed me into the room, ahead of him. The sunlight was streaming through the windowpane and catching the rainbow colours of the mobile hearts hanging from the ceiling above my bed.

'Remove your skirt now,' he spoke abruptly without ceremony or concern. I was sobbing with fear and apprehension by this time but knew better than to disobey him more than I had done already. He was as angry as he could be and I knew that I was in big trouble. I did as I was told and removed my red tartan check pleated skirt as slowly as I could in a feeble attempt to delay the inevitable.

I carefully folded my skirt and placed it over the back of the white wooden chair by my desk. I knew that if I didn't do this properly then Daddy would be even more cross with me. He hates mess and untidiness and frequent beatings for leaving my clothes lying about have taught me to always fold them neatly no matter what the circumstances.

When I had done this, with a racing heart I turned round to face Daddy. He had sat himself down on the edge of the bed. Behind him were an army of my toys all neatly lined up along the far wall. The seven dwarves were directly seated behind Daddy and I could see a couple of dwarves either side of Daddy. My toys were sitting in a line on the pink and white gingham duvet, witnesses to my childhood. Of course, in pride of place, allowed to sleep inside the duvet with his head on the pillow no less, was Pooh Bear himself.

I noticed that Daddy had already removed his belt and had placed it beside him on the bed. 'Do you know why I am going to punish you, Lucy?' I did know why. I knew exactly what I had done to deserve this. I had been in the middle of throwing a temper tantrum at my mother when he had arrived home earlier than usual and caught me screaming and shouting at her.

I had wanted to watch a programme on television but she had said no. I was supposed to be doing my homework instead. Because I could not watch the television programme I had sat myself down in protest on the sofa and refused to do any of my set schoolwork. I sat there screaming and yelling, trying to wear her down, to make Mummy give in, when Daddy walked through the door. I had been making such a fuss that neither of us had even heard his key in the lock or the sound of the door closing shut behind him. He came over to where I was seated on the sofa and demanded silence.

Now he was demanding that I walk over to him. I did as I was told and stood contritely before Daddy. I was genuinely sorry for my behaviour and hoped that he would see this and not be so angry with me. he took hold of my sore arm again, which was still very red with fingerprint bruises already appearing from where he had held me earlier. He quickly and without warning pulled me down across his lap. I closed my eyes tightly, fearing the fate that was about to befall me.

'Lucy … Lucy … it's me. You're okay. Wake up, kiddo, wake up, it's just a dream. You're having a bad dream, kiddo.' Slowly I was roused from this nightmare by both Adam and Bryony who were beside my bed looking down at me. I woke up in a real fright and sat straight up in the bed. I pulled my knees up to my chin and felt the side of my head with my hand – just to see if I had knocked my head or not. My head was not hurting but my face was covered with tears nonetheless. It was only a dream. Bryony sat down beside me and put her arm round my shoulder. I shrugged from her in order to pull myself away from this embrace. She respected my feelings and let go. Adam looked concerned but at a loss as to whether he was welcome there or not. I wept for some time and got through several tissues, which Bryony passed to me. But I refused to discuss my dream with either of them, knowing full well that they wouldn't understand. If I told them they would hate me for sure, and they seemed to like me. I really didn't want to risk that. Letting people know how bad I am would be a big mistake. Aside from this who would believe me anyway? No – there was too much to consider.

After a short while Bryony and Adam both left me alone in my bed. I had stopped crying and was just laying there playing with Pooh Bear. He wears a little red T-shirt, which is removable, so when I haven't got much else to do in bed I slowly undress him, and then I dress him again before he catches a cold. I usually hold him high up in the air as well and pretend that he is flying freely through the air without any help from me whatsoever. I was doing this when Elaine appeared, her tall shadow blocking out some of the light that usually shines in from the corridor.

'Do you need my help?' I softly enquired. 'Yeah, if…' Without allowing Elaine to finish her sentence I said that I would be right there. I leapt willingly out of my bed and followed Elaine into her 'cell' where we stripped the soggy sheets and remade the bed with fresh crisp sheets between us. As usual nothing much was said while we did this. Elaine looked gaunt and tired, especially in the dim light from the corridor. I tried to look cheery, as though nothing much had happened that night to me.

'Lucy, do you wanna talk about those dreams? I am your friend you know, you can tell me if you want to …'

I scowled at her for even suggesting that there was anything that I needed to talk about. 'Look, Elaine, they are just dreams that's all. A dream. Martin Luther King had a famous one if I remember rightly.' Feeling the need to close this subject as quickly as possible, I insisted, 'There's nothing to talk about, believe me, I don't even remember them when I wake up.' Of course this wasn't strictly true but I knew that it would be the most effective way of getting her off my back. If I couldn't remember when I woke up, then I couldn't be pushed to talk about what I couldn't remember, right? Stroke of genius, I thought.

'All right girls … if you've finished in here then you really ought to get back into your beds now. Otherwise you'll both be too tired to concentrate at school tomorrow,' Bryony gently informed us.

I went back into the dorm area after saying goodnight to Elaine. It was extremely silent throughout the building. Siobhan and Rebecca both had their doors closed, as they had been asleep a long time. Clearly my nightmare had not disturbed them, so that was some small relief. The dim light from the nurses' office only served to reinforce the darkness elsewhere.

I pressed the little button on my watch and it lit up the digital time: 5.15 a.m. Not too long until 8 a.m. then I can get up for breakfast. I tried to think about the breakfast that I was going to eat. I tried to picture in my mind crisp Cornflakes and hot buttered toast dripping with as much jam as I would like, but somehow in spite of myself, my thoughts kept dragging me back to some other place. Somewhere less pleasant, but more powerful in its lure.

In spite of all attempts to ignore it, the noise and the screams filled my head regardless. Each time I closed my eyes I kept returning to where my dream had ended earlier. Neither my unconscious nor my waking mind could defeat the power of that memory. Within that one recollection were crystallised a thousand other memories all taking refuge in the sanctuary behind it. As if by being poured into one they could be diluted and less real.

The firm pressure of Daddy's free arm around my waist was keeping me in place over his lap. I could feel his legs beneath me cutting into my chest with each movement I made. The more that I fought and tried to wriggle free, Daddy's grip only tightened. He waited until I stopped trying to escape. I laid still, realising that I was only adding to my discomfort through fighting and wriggling.

Daddy reminded me of the tantrum that I was guilty of. My unacceptable behaviour was the cause of all this. I left him no choice. 'You need to learn how to behave.' With those words I felt the sting of the first smack. The intensity of the pain increased as Daddy repeatedly smacked me. His belt landed hard across my bottom in quick successive smacks. Occasionally he would miss his actual target and catch instead the tops of my legs, with the strap winding its way around my thighs leaving marks like thick tails. Daddy continued to punish me relentlessly, immune to my tears, screams and protests.

After a short while, I became aware that my underwear was being completely removed. My white cotton knickers had been my only protection against the harshness of the belt strap and now Daddy was taking that thin layer of protection away. When he had removed them, he continued to beat me.

43

Only this time the belt strap was landing on my bare, already marked, skin. I had no protection whatsoever and I felt terrified. 'Daddy, please stop, please ...' In between sobs, I begged him for mercy but received none. My cries were ignored as if unheard. He continued to smack me. Defenceless and sorry though I was, it made no difference. I had misbehaved and this was the consequence.

Then, without any indication that he was going to stop, he did. He ordered me to stand up. I slowly picked myself up from his lap and stood repentantly before him. I put my thumb in my mouth to comfort myself. With my free hand I instinctively touched my bottom in a vain attempt to stop it from hurting and to protect it from any further smacks.

Daddy remained seated on my bed. He ordered me to look at him, as my eyes had been focused downwards onto the pink fluffy carpet. I instantly obeyed him. He asked if I thought I had learned my lesson now. I nodded affirmatively while whimpering, 'Yes'.

'Good, that's all I wanted to hear.' With that he stood up, holding the belt in his hand. I trembled when Daddy moved to get up from the bed. He ordered me to get into bed. He said that if I were not in bed in five minutes flat then he would punish me again. But the next time, he assured me, the punishment would be much harder.

As soon as Daddy had left my room and closed the bedroom door behind him I leant across my bed and rescued Pooh Bear. I held him close to me. With each movement I made, the stinging seemed to worsen. I hugged Pooh Bear tight, telling him that everything would be OK and promising that I would be a good girl from now on so that Daddy would never have to punish us again.

Remembering Daddy's warning I hurriedly removed my white vest and changed into my nightdress. As I pulled my favourite pink nightdress over my head I flinched when the soft cotton came into contact with my sore skin.

Glancing over my shoulder into the free-standing mirror I tentatively lifted up the back of my nightdress. Thick angry red strap marks across my bottom and the tops of my legs were etched on to my otherwise unbroken pale skin. The colourful bruising was even more vivid against the rest of my milky white skin, ranging from the darkest of purples to deep red and then less severely to lighter pink stripes where Daddy had only landed the strap a few times. All over, my bottom burned and stung. The slightest of movement caused fresh pain.

Seeing the marks only served to exacerbate my distress. The visible marks of my punishment reminded me of Daddy's anger and of my own repeated failure to be good. I tried so hard to be a good girl but I always fell far short of the target. I always made Daddy angry because I just couldn't behave myself like Kara did.

It wasn't too long before I heard Daddy's footsteps on the stairs. I knew that he was heading straight for my room. I hurriedly climbed into my bed and had no choice other than to lie on my tummy, holding Pooh Bear close to me.

There was nowhere that I could go to get away from Daddy. Every friend of the family loves my mother and father. They are well-respected and people come to them for advice and help when they've got problems with their own children. That's probably why Daddy is so strict with us all, because he has to set an example, I suppose. But then again, we're never allowed to tell anyone about these beatings … or the other stuff, so how can that be setting an example for anybody? Daddy doesn't exactly advertise the fact that we're so naughty and that he has to punish us with his belt strap.

I did used to try so hard to be a good girl, but nothing I did was ever good enough so I gave up trying. That's when I started to go really wild, when I tried to kill myself too. There doesn't seem much point in living when you're as miserable as I am so I tried to cut my wrists and bleed to death – several times. My parents don't really talk about those incidents, though. It's like they never happened. It's kind of like a lot never happened in my home. I mean, a lot never happened that did actually happen, if you know what I mean. I don't want to think about that stuff while I'm in here though. I'm getting a break now, and so I suppose that I ought to make the most of it before I'm sent back home.

I've got to get home as soon as I possibly can though, because Kara is there alone – she needs me to help her, I know that she does. She's only eleven and she's going to need her sister. If they don't let me out of here soon I'll have to make a run for it I guess.

Eventually as I lost my self further and further in the midst of my tormenting, terrorising thoughts I noticed the sun beginning to shine in through the cracks in the curtains which do not close properly where they are supposed to meet at the top. I checked the time again and saw that it was 7.32 a.m. so I decided to get up and take a shower, before the other girls would be woken at 8 a.m. It made sense to avoid the queue, especially as I had been awake for hours anyway. I did feel tired, but relieved that sleep hadn't won me over twice in one night.

From the view through the window the day outside looked as though it were promising to be hot and dry. In light of this I chose to wear my light pink summer dress with the bows that tied up at each side of the dress. On my feet I wore my black leather patent shoes with the buckles across the middle. These are my favourite shoes.

I managed to find Adam before he left Redfield after his night shift was over. 'Do you mind tying my hair up, please?' I asked.

'Of course not,' he replied and quickly, almost kindly, tied my ponytail with the pink ribbon which I handed to him. 'There you go,' Adam said when he had finished. 'You look very pretty. I would be proud to have a daughter like you.'

46

That statement stopped me dead in my tracks. 'Would you? … I mean, really … would you? Do you mean it or are you just saying it for a joke?' Without hesitating, Adam insisted that he meant every word. 'It would be an honour. I would be very proud if I had a daughter like you,' he reiterated. He looked me straight in the eyes too, so that it would have been harder for him to be teasing, I guess. I smiled gratefully and walked off to take my place at the dining table in time to join the other girls for breakfast. Little did I know how much I was going to need to remember those words to find the strength to face the task ahead of me that day.

Chapter 4

Breakfast was relatively quiet for Redfield on a weekday morning. The day nurses were back on duty, with Charlotte and Harriet, who was the more senior nurse out of the two. The nurses sat at the breakfast table with us girls and drank coffee while we ate our Cornflakes and toast. It is good here at mealtimes as we are allowed to eat as much as we like. Seriously, we can just help ourselves to as many bowls of cereal as we feel like and the nurses never stop us or anything. We have to be in school at 9 a.m. though, so I guess that if you were still eating and all at nine then they'd pack you off to school pretty sharp. But that's only so you'd get to school on time. With the food they are really generous. Unlike at home, when I often went to bed feeling terribly hungry as a result of making one or both of my parents cross with me so that they sent me up to bed without any food. That is not an uncommon occurrence in my family home.

My first class was Home Economics with Gill. But the teacher knew and understood how much I hated learning to make marmalade and other such tasks. After some persuasion I was given special permission to sit at a table away from the kitchen area and read through my French school book from Harrington High. I played on the fact that there were no adequate French lessons at Sea House School as I argued that I needed all the private practice I could get. They didn't really care anyway – just so long as I was in the classroom doing something that wasn't going to get me into trouble, then they were pretty cool about it. I told you, this isn't like any real school.

Siobhan and Rebecca were also in the Home Economics group with me and they were involved with preparing their lumpy orange marmalade mixture when Charlotte popped her head in to the schoolroom and asked Gill if she could have a private word. I kind of knew in an instant that it would be about me, even though I didn't have any direct evidence for this assumption other than this hunch that I somehow get when I know that I am being talked about. The psychiatrist that I have to see here once a month told me ages ago that I suffer from paranoia. But I reckon he's just jealous that he doesn't know when he's the one being talked about.

Gill came back through the thick white double classroom doors with Charlotte by her side. Gill put me in mind of Florence Nightingale with her long white chiffon summer dress flowing around her as she walked. Charlotte wore her usual tight blue jeans and rainbow-coloured top. The psychiatric nurses always tried to dress really cool, but usually failed miserably because they often looked so out of place in their own clothes. For a moment both women looked at me as though I were some wounded rabbit about to be slaughtered.

Gill walked right past me and on to the kitchen area without saying anything to me directly. Charlotte approached the desk where I sat with French books scattered before me. She asked me very gently if I would leave my books at my desk for a short while and go with her. I noticed the demand as opposed to the request in this statement, so I complied without any fuss or protest. I got up from my chair and followed Charlotte out of the classroom, wondering what it was that I could have done wrong. I thought that maybe they had decided to put me on punishment after all for scratching Rebecca's face last night. My face flushed at

49

the thought of having to go back to school wearing my pink pyjamas.

We had walked right out of the school building into the open sunshine before Charlotte even told me where we were actually going. 'Lucy, I'm taking you to see Mr Williams. He's expecting you now.'

I thought about this for a moment then said in earnest, 'But I never see Mr Williams on a Tuesday – my therapy is always on a Thursday! Why am I seeing him today?' I persisted in asking Charlotte to reveal to me what this was all about. Why was I being summoned to see my therapist at this strange hour and on a Tuesday? Charlotte remained obstinate in her silence. I had no doubt that she knew exactly what this was all about but was refusing to discuss it with me.

We arrived at Jarvis House and at Mr Williams's office within a few minutes as the buildings were situated so near to each other. As soon as we arrived he stepped outside of his office to greet us. There was no leaving me next to the oxygen plant this time. He thanked Charlotte for bringing me across to him in the manner in which a more senior official addresses someone of lower rank. Mr Williams was clearly trying so very hard not to be patronising that he ended up by doing just that. Charlotte took it all in her stride and asked if she ought to wait for me or not. To my surprise Mr Williams suggested that this would be wise, and offered Charlotte the seat next to the plant. Only then did he invite me into his office.

I followed him, watching his khaki trousers and his brown shoes as he walked over to the small black leather chair beside his desk. He sat down with apparent unease. I noticed that he was wearing a different shirt to any that I had seen before. This one had little flecks of brown amongst the overall beige colour. I wondered to myself if he had even noticed his own shirt. I was about to ask him this when he began speaking.

'Lucy, is there anything that you want to tell me about?' Mr Williams fired this question straight at me. I paced up and down the room for a while, looking first at the door, then out of the window, then back towards the door, then out of the window. There was no need to sit down, as Mr Williams had not insisted on this. He seemed to understand my anxiety and the need to walk it off.

'No, not really,' I responded hesitantly. There were so many thoughts whizzing through my mind but none of them seemed relevant to speak about. I wondered if this line of questioning had anything to do with my nightmares, which admittedly had been more frequent of late.

'I have something that I must tell you about, Lucy. You might want to sit down for this. But before I start it's really important that you realise that I am on your side in this. I only want to help you and that's what I am here for.' The serious tone of his voice worried and alarmed me instantly. He had never before addressed me with such formality or with so much fear in his eyes.

'OK, what is it?' I questioned him right back, feeling infected by his own fear. The tension in the air between us was so great that had it not been for the multitude of plants scattered around his tiny office I probably would have suffocated right there and then.

'There was a case conference held at your school, Lucy. I was invited to attend as I am your therapist and your subject teachers were also asked to be present.' Panic gripped my mind and body as he said these words. I knew what was coming, but I was hoping with every last vestige of hope in my body that the words I dreaded to hear the most were not going to be said.

'Your German teacher Ms Friedman said at the conference that you had disclosed to her some months ago that you were being sexually abused by your father.'

I slumped into the pink armchair, no longer able to find

the strength to remain standing. Horrified and panic-stricken I demanded to know everything that he knew. 'How? Why? … Why were you all talking about me? My mother … what will she think of me? She will hate me … Daddy – he's going to kill me. He will really kill me, Mr Williams; he'll kill me … and Mummy too. What can I do? I've got to speak to Mummy, I have to tell her that I love her. I have to. Let me ring her now. May I please …' And so the words came rushing out. Sentence after broken sentence falling over each other. Words to undo the damage done by other words. Somehow these words were just too weak to annul the potency of those other words, spoken at some other more trusting time.

The world as I knew it had crashed around me in a lightning moment. I sat rigid in the pink armchair and the words dried up as quickly as they had poured out in desperation. All was truly lost. My family, my hopes, my life. Mr Williams had watched me in attentive silence throughout this entire emotional outburst. He had seen my reaction, the desperate fear in my eyes, and the pleas for it all not to be happening. For the first time I had let down my emotional guard in his presence.

The betrayal by Ms Friedman cut me the deepest. Betrayal after endless betrayal. First Daddy, then Mummy, even by her unknowing silence. Then Ms Friedman. Damn her for betraying me. I had told her the greatest secret of my life in confidence. I had risked my life in saying a single word about what was going on at home, and she had chosen to repay that trust in her by putting me on the line like this. She may as well have fired the bullet through my heart on that very same day I gave her my confidence. Not only was I being punished by being sent to Redfield, I was now no longer considered worthy of the promises she had made to me on that fateful day.

Ms Friedman had noticed during German class the constant bandages that I wore around my wrist and had invited me to talk to her on several occasions. Often when we were left to do our composition exercises and the rest of the class were quietly talking amongst themselves, she would approach my solitary desk and ask me if everything was all right at home. My answer would invariably be, 'Yes, of course,' but she would continue to ask me if there was anything at all on my mind that I would like to talk about. I always said that there was nothing that I needed to talk about, but she knew right away that that was the biggest load of rubbish she'd ever heard. On one particular occasion, after I had cut my wrist severely the night before and not bothered to change the bloodied bandage with a fresh clean one before school, Ms Friedman called me into her office at break-time.

Ms Friedman, being head of languages, had quite a large office to herself. There were bookcases along the length of each of the walls and masses and masses of books. I used to look at those books hoping that one day I would be able to read them and learn as much as Ms Friedman – but not necessarily German though. I've always been more interested in literature and art, and Ms Friedman had books on those subjects also.

After inviting me to sit down opposite her while she sat at her large brown desk, I hesitated before I actually sat down. I felt trapped – caught out, as though I knew already that Ms Friedman was about to confront me with the greatest secret of my life. In a desperate attempt to avoid eye contact with this teacher who had made it her business to intrude upon my family life, I noticed the neat piles of crisp white papers stacked along the back of the formidable oak desk. Her pens were also neatly lined up along the left side of the desk, and I was wondering how she managed to keep her desk so tidy and all, when she suddenly spoke, saying that she *knew* there was an ongoing problem for me at home. She just came right out and said it, broke the silence with that statement alone.

I was stunned by Ms Friedman's knowledge when I had not told her anything. She didn't even ask if there were problems this time, but declared to me that there was one. I denied this instantly, but she told me that in her experience of life, young girls don't cut their wrists over anything small. Ms Friedman looked at me from out of her small gold-framed glasses with her austere German expression. With her dark brown hair pinned up high on top of her head and the long pencil-style black skirt which could not conceal the thinness of her legs, matched with the same grey blouse that she always wore, she did look intimidating. I wriggled uncomfortably in my seat for a bit, partly because her confrontation made me feel uneasy as well as afraid, and partly due to the fact that she was reminding me, without realising it herself of course, of the events at home the night before.

Confidentially she told me that when she was a child she had suffered problems with her father and that she could see I was having similar problems. Well, I still suck my thumb even in class and I am thirteen – maybe that gave it away, I don't know. Ms Friedman assured me that if I told her about anything then it wouldn't go any further than the four walls of her office. She promised. She promised. She said she understood the need for secrecy. It was imperative that Daddy never discovered that this had even been acknowledged by another person, otherwise he would carry out his threats to kill me.

With this thought rushing through my mind, I promptly collapsed into sobs that shook my whole body. Ms Friedman, in spite of her frightening appearance, was dead kind to me at this point. She brought a tissue over to me and wiped the tears from my face herself – I mean, with her own hands holding the now soggy tissue she continued to wipe my eyes. That's the only time in my life that anyone has ever wiped away my tears.

Eventually I managed to stop crying, but Ms Friedman, she

didn't leave me or anything like that. She stayed right there virtually kneeling beside my chair while she put her arm right round my shoulder. When I regained enough composure to be able to speak with clarity I stressed the urgent need for secrecy. In spite of my fear I poured out the details of Daddy's threats to kill me, Mummy and also Kara if I dared to breathe a word of this to anybody.

I tried to make Ms Friedman understand that Daddy really did mean this, that there was no doubt in my mind that if I broke the silence I would see my family murdered. I didn't really care so much for my own life, but I sure did not want to see Mummy die or Kara. Just because *I* am a bad girl, Mummy and Kara should not have to pay the price for that, I reasoned.

'Please understand, Miss, please don't tell anyone – especially Daddy – please don't tell Daddy that you know about this. He told me that he would deny it anyway, and everyone will hate me for saying such things. Everyone will know what a bad girl I am, Miss – that's what Daddy said too ...' I collapsed again into sobs which hurt my whole body.

I felt dirty and unclean before this kind, caring teacher who was showing me warmth and compassion that I did not deserve in light of the terrible things I had done. The sun streamed in through the office window at this point, and almost blinded by its penetrating rays I lowered my gaze and looked at the floor. Ms Friedman was facing me so that the window and the sun were behind her. This meant that although she could see me I was still unable to look at her. In point of fact this made it a whole lot easier to cope with the situation that Ms Friedman had placed me in with this unexpected confrontation. If I didn't look directly at her then I felt that she wasn't really seeing me either – in my wretched miserable state. The disgust that I felt towards myself inside of me was so overwhelming that I was sure that it oozed out of me in plain view of all those who came near me.

'I will not tell anyone about this Lucy; not unless you want me to.' Those were Ms Friedman's very own words, said firmly and with apparent conviction. In my innocence I believed her. I had no option but to believe this teacher who had taken me into her office, taken me into her arms and wiped my tears away with the hands of a mother who loves her child more than anything else in the world. 'All I ask is that you will come to talk to me instead of cutting your wrist. I don't want to see you hurting yourself any more.' She waited for me to respond to this request, but I really could not think of anything to say. I cut my wrist with the hope that I would find my artery and kill myself. Well, that's what I told myself anyway. I thought of it as Russian Roulette. If I died I wouldn't care, because it would mean that I would be free from this pain that I had to live through. Now I was being asked to give up my only hope for release.

Of course, talking to Ms Friedman about what Daddy actually did to me would be entirely out of the question. She clearly knew that I was being abused but even at that point I did not reveal any specific details to her. She asked if the abuse were sexual and my tears told her that it was. Yet when she asked if I were also being physically abused, I said no. I didn't know then that being beaten with a belt as a punishment for misbehaviour constituted physical abuse. I thought that my father had every right to do this to me. After all, he told me on enough occasions that he did it because he loves me and wants to make me a better person. 'You don't always want to be a bad girl do you?' he would ask. Obviously I said that I didn't and so I accepted that this punishment was for my own good. After all, as my father he must know what is best for me.

I left Ms Friedman's office that day feeling an immense sense of relief. Relief over the fact that I was no longer so completely alone with this terrible secret, relief regarding the fact that she had sincerely promised me that this information would go no further. Ms Friedman really did seem to understand that I loved my family and I could not bear to lose them. But more than this I felt for the first time since Daddy had started hurting me that someone actually cared about me. In spite of how bad I was, my teacher's reaction certainly did not match my father's belief that I would be scorned and despised in the event of someone finding out about 'our secret'. Quite the opposite seemed to be the case; this in itself took me by surprise.

I trusted Ms Friedman and I looked on her with the utmost respect from that day forward. Even German classes became more appealing because I knew that I would be seeing her again. This teacher, this woman who had erased my tears from my very own face would be there at the front of the class. Often she asked me back to her office at break-times where she would bring me some orange juice. We never again discussed my family circumstances but I knew that if I had wanted to – or more appropriately been able to – then she would certainly have been there more than willing to listen.

This made her betrayal of my secret all the more painful and difficult to take on board. For months Ms Friedman really did not reveal anything to anyone, as indeed she had promised me would be the case. Then suddenly, when I am incarcerated for being 'emotionally disturbed', she deems me to be less of the person that I was before. That sure was immensely difficult to understand.

Mr Williams seemed to understand that I was feeling this way because he said in some sort of half-hearted defence of Ms Friedman, 'She only spoke out because she thought that it was in your best interest for her to do so, Lucy. I was there … I assure you that it was a well thought-out decision. The school was really worried about you, especially after expelling you like that. After all your academic record is …' – and he paused at this point to check that I was paying attention to his words and not lost in some inner reverie of my own – 'excellent. That's why they called this case conference in the first place, to try to get to the root of your disturbance. They want you back at Harrington High just as soon as you are well again.'

They want me back. I mulled over those words and laughed. 'But my parents won't want me back, will they? They'll never want me again. That is, if they don't kill me first anyway. Daddy will never forgive me … It's not true, Mr Williams. It's not true, so don't even tell Daddy that I told on him or anything … please?' I blurted out hysterically.

Mr Williams paused to allow me time to reflect on what I had said and to calm down a little. 'I'm not the one who is going to deal with your father, Lucy. It is not my responsibility to do that. However I must inform you that the police have already arrested him. They have taken him down to the local police station earlier this morning to be questioned.'

After a few moments of stunned silence I looked up at Mr Williams and made direct eye contact for the first time that morning. It was strange, because I felt simultaneously free and trapped. Almost as though life could go either way for me right now, and I was the only one who could make any sort of decision which would influence my destiny.

'Daddy … has been arrested …' I repeated in complete disbelief. 'Will he be put …' I stumbled over my words at this point, afraid that to say them would make them happen but still needing to know the answer, '… in jail?'

Mr Williams quietly explained to me that no, Daddy would not be put in jail in the immediate future at least. That even if Daddy admits to abusing me he would still get a court hearing where his fate would be decided. Of course, Daddy would never admit to that. He even told me himself that if I ever told on him then everyone would know what a bad girl I am and that he would deny doing it. Daddy said that no one would ever believe me or would want me any more, and that

Mummy would hate me. When I was younger – about seven – he threatened to kill Mummy and then me if I told her what we did together. So I kept silent for all these years.

Mr Williams looked at me with compassion and tenderness in his eyes as he further explained that the police were waiting to interview me.

'Me? The police ... are here for me? Am I going to jail, am I in trouble? Are they taking me to see Daddy?'

After my barrage of confused questions ceased, Mr Williams said that I was certainly not in any trouble. He assured me that the police lady waiting to interview me was very kind and that he could make this claim with authority on the grounds that he knew her personally. She was trained to talk to children under these 'circumstances' and that she would be very gentle with me. 'You have nothing to fear, I promise you. There is a male police officer with her, but he won't question you, OK? He'll just be present, that's all, kiddo.'

I liked the way in which Mr Williams called me 'kiddo'. Right now it was especially reassuring.

'Would you like me to sit in with you while you're questioned? I'm afraid that someone from this place has to be present at these interviews. It's the procedure. But it doesn't have to be me. Either Harriet or myself can sit with you, whoever you feel more comfortable with. But it has to be a senior member of staff.'

Without realising that I was even consenting to be interviewed, I settled for Harriet to be present with me.

'Mr Williams,' I tentatively asked, 'do you hate me now ... you know about ... this stuff?' Tears trickled down my face in spite of my best efforts to keep them inside.

'There's no reason on this earth why I would hate you, Lucy. You haven't done anything wrong, kiddo. There isn't one person who would think differently than I do, either.' He handed me a tissue as he spoke, and he seemed to speak with apparent sincerity. 'I have known for a long while, Lucy. I was just waiting until you were ready to speak about whatever has been going on, that's all. That's my job; I have to respect your right to discuss whatever you wish…' he broke off at this point as, taking the tissue from him I interrupted, 'But Mr Williams, do you not think that I am bad at all, not in any way? Or disgusting? You can tell me the truth, as I know it already.'

After a few seconds of painful silence in which I almost held my breath, Mr Williams reaffirmed his earlier claim that he could not see how I could be in any way to blame. 'Therefore how could I think that you are bad, Lucy? You have not done anything bad. No doubt you have had bad things done to you, but you are not responsible for that.'

I was no longer listening to Mr Williams at this point. The reality of the impending police interview was making itself more keenly felt.

'I've had an idea … If I deny that what I said to Ms Friedman is true then will Daddy still be in trouble anyway? If I say that I lied will they let him go home from the police station? … Do you think that my parents will want me back again, Mr Williams? I mean, do you think that they will forgive me if I say it is not true?'

After a moment's thought Mr Williams told me that it would be entirely within my rights to deny any earlier statements that I had made to Ms Friedman. Although in point of fact I had never disclosed any details to her, so there couldn't be too much evidence for the police to go on anyway.

'But then will everyone here hate me and think that I am just a liar?' I was completely damned, no matter which way I turned. All those things that Daddy had warned me of would now come true. I felt alone, without a single person in the world who would support or even be able to love me again.

'It happens all the time that children retract allegations of sexual abuse, for various reasons. You would not be the first one to choose to do that, Lucy. No one here will be surprised, or condemn you, whatever you decide to tell the police.' Mr Williams looked at me kindly, and with a gentle voice he repeated his earlier assertion that he was there for me and that he was on my side. 'Whatever you decide to say, Lucy, I will support you.'

'Are you sure?' I desperately wanted reassurance that I could make this all go away just by claiming that it really wasn't true after all, that I had lied because I am the bad girl that my father is always telling me I am. After all, he may never forgive me anyway for breaking our silence, but I had to give it a try. I knew that with all the strength that I could summon up, I had to begin to repair some of the damage I had done to my family. I didn't want to be separated from my brother and sister or even my parents for that matter. Neither could I live with myself if Daddy were permanently taken away from our home – and all because of me. Regardless of what they did to me, they are after all the only parents that I have in the world. Without them I would be truly alone. I needed them to love me and to want me and I knew that I had to do everything I could in order to regain their acceptance and hopefully win their forgiveness.

Chapter 5

'We really ought to be thinking about getting this interview over and done with as the police officers have been here waiting to speak to you all morning.' When saying this, Mr Williams picked at some imaginary fluff on his shirt as though he felt nervous himself.

For a brief second I wanted to run out of the room and as far away from Redfield as possible. But I knew that I would not get very far with Charlotte sitting outside the therapist's office. Not only that, it would be an extremely long run just to get to the exit, as the grounds are extensive. My heart probably wouldn't be able to make it anyhow.

'Sure,' I replied, 'I guess I have no choice, right? But you do know, don't you, that I will be denying everything.' After a pause, I added despondently, 'I have to …'

'I do accept your decision, Lucy; we will discuss your feelings about this some more at our next therapy session. But really you must face the police now. You seem to be a lot calmer, so it might be an idea to talk with them while you are feeling stronger in yourself.'

That was a joke – I didn't feel that I had any strength left in my entire body. Each time Mr Williams mentioned the word 'police' I felt as though my whole body were disintegrating. However I relented to the wishes of those in charge of me and agreed to see the police as soon as Harriet arrived to sit in the interview room with us.

Trembling from head to foot, the loud knock at Mr Williams's door terrified me even more. It was only Harriet, who had been telephoned by my therapist and requested to come over to Jarvis House to accompany me. She smiled a great beaming smile at me as though it were intended to reassure me that none of this was really all that bad. I had lost my entire family, my whole world was smashed into thousands of shards, and all that Harriet could do about it was to grin when looking at me.

'Are you ready to meet the police lady now?' Harriet asked as she looked down at me. She is tall – about six foot – and quite lean so she looked a bit like a giant from where I was sitting crouched low in the armchair. Her hair is really short and silvery grey and I'd guess that her age is somewhere in the late forties. Because she always wears trousers with shirts, her appearance immediately strikes one as being quite masculine.

I got up from the chair and walked towards the door as an indication that I was as ready as I would ever be. Harriet followed closely behind me as we left Mr Williams in his office. He mumbled something that sounded like 'Good luck' as we were leaving, but I didn't respond.

Harriet led the way along the white corridor at the end of which we turned right and walked slowly up a small flight of stairs. My hand held tightly to the battered grey handrail as I climbed each stair. When we reached the top of the staircase we walked along another shorter corridor, also with white walls, that led to another room. Before we entered the designated interview room, Harriet informed me that she was there to support me personally, and that both the police officers and the staff at Redfield Unit would accept whatever I chose to say. I nodded as a sign that I understood what she was endeavouring to explain. My body was literally frozen with fear, and I shivered slightly as Harriet knocked on the door before she led me in to confront my fate.

The large airy room looked like a schoolroom or a playroom – it really could have been used for either of these purposes. There were lots of brightly painted posters all over the otherwise white walls which caught my attention immediately due to the strong vibrant colours and the vast amount of amateur paintings which were on display everywhere. Harriet let me take in my new surroundings before she introduced me to the police officers who were already present.

There was a fairly tall man standing in the corner by the door as though he were trying to look inconspicuous, but clearly failing in this task. He had on a white shirt with black trousers and looked very much like a police officer. Harriet introduced me but I immediately forgot his name. I quietly said 'Hi', and then turned my attention to the seated police lady who was clearly the officer who was about to question me. There were two other vacant chairs placed opposite the police lady who was introduced by Harriet as being 'Police Detective Adams'. However I was immediately spoken to reassuringly by the said police lady who told me that I could call her Pam.

Harriet invited me to sit down and so I took my place reluctantly in the grey plastic chair she offered to me. Harriet then sat down in the chair beside me. After a few moments' silence in which we all seemed to be looking at each other, Harriet finally spoke. I was told not to worry about stopping the questioning at any point if I felt that it was overly distressing. 'Take all the time that you need, Lucy. We are not in any rush here, OK?'

They may not have been in any rush to get this over with, but I certainly was. I just wanted to deny the whole thing and get out of there. In the back of my mind I kept seeing images of my father locked up in a police cell, alone and angry with me.

Then the police lady turned her attention towards me –

although I had been painfully aware that she had not taken her eyes off me from the moment I had entered the room. She smiled and tried to look as unthreatening as possible. Her legs were crossed and her black skirt came just below her knees. She had lovely blonde hair that was tied back from her pale but pretty face. She looked as though she were around thirty. I shifted nervously in my chair and felt my entire body tense up when she finally addressed me.

When I eventually found the courage to meet her gaze I sensed that her piercing blue eyes bore right into my soul. I knew that this lady was going to know in an instant if I told her a lie. 'Lucy, I know this is difficult for you but I am here to ask you some questions. I am used to speaking to children who have been hurt by adults in all sorts of ways. There is nothing that you could tell me that would shock me. I have probably heard it all before anyway. So please tell me everything that you can. I am here to help you by seeing that any abuse that might be happening to you will be stopped. We want to protect you, Lucy. Nobody is here to punish you. Do you understand this?'

'Yes, I do ...' I forced myself to meet that penetrating gaze for the second time that afternoon.

'We understand that you have made serious allegations of sexual abuse against you by your father. It is our intention to question you regarding the information that you shared with Ms Friedman whom I understand is your German teacher.'

That was rich, considering that I had not actually shared any details with Ms Friedman on any occasion. All that she could possibly know is that this thing they referred to as 'sexual abuse' had been occurring. I was determined not to allow myself to be tricked by these police officers. I had a strong feeling inside of my stomach that was telling me I was the one on trial here.

The police lady paused for a moment to see if I would respond to her statement or not. When she saw that I was not about to speak to her willingly, she asked me directly, 'Is it true that your father has hurt you in a sexual way? Has he touched your body anywhere against your will?'

I was too afraid to speak, my heart was racing so fast that I thought it must be clearly audible to those present in the room. All eyes there were focused on me seated in the little plastic grey chair with my eyes lowered to the floor. I noticed that the buckle across my left black patent leather shoe was undone. There are three holes in which to place the metal buckle but the leather around the last hole had become torn and so my buckle had undone itself.

Noticing my inattention to her questions the police officer reiterated, 'Did your father ever touch you anywhere inappropriate?' The question broke through into the silence and demolished the wall of protection that I had constructed for myself. It was too difficult not to think about these things when questions like this were being thrown at me.

Shame rose up from within me as I recalled bedtimes at home. Why didn't I stop him? Why didn't I ever stop him? The same question ran itself through my mind like a stuck record. How could Daddy even be blamed for this? After all, it was me he was doing it to, so clearly it was my fault anyway. *I made him do it.* I made him do it. If only I were a good enough girl then I am sure that Daddy wouldn't hurt me anyway. Of course Daddy knew best. How could this police lady drag me in here and try to suggest that Daddy was even wrong? He could not be wrong, he is my father. I love him because he is my father. No, that's wrong. I love him because he loves me. I just love him.

With these thoughts racing through my mind, I tentatively ventured a reply to the police lady's questions. 'Daddy has never hurt me. Never. Ms Friedman … she lied … I mean … I lied … to her…' The words faltered as they came out of my mouth; my eyes were still fixed firmly upon the grey linoleum floor. 'Really, none of it's true. Daddy would never do bad things to me. I lied. I lied. I lied!' I virtually screamed out these last words.

Harriet lent forward in her chair to place her bony, gentle old hand on my shoulder. 'It's all right, Lucy, we understand.'

After a few moments' silence in which I was given time to recollect my composure the police lady's questions continued. 'Why did you lie to your teacher, Lucy? In my experience very few children do actually lie about these things.'

'I lied because I am a bad person.' I had to think fast, as I had not expected this question. Why had I lied? I didn't know what reason there could be, but it was evident that the police officer was not going to relent in her questioning. Thinking fast, I just blurted out the first thing that came into my mind. 'I was angry with Daddy … he punished me one time for bad behaviour and sent me to my room. I was angry about having to go to my room. So the very next day I lied to the teacher about him because I hated him.'

'Do you remember exactly when this was?' The police lady was clearly trying to catch me out, so I simply said, 'No, of course not, it was such a long time ago now.'

I waited for her to shout at me or to arrest me or something but she didn't. I glanced up quickly at her pretty face and noticed that she made eye contact with the male police officer who was still standing in the exact same spot in the corner. He did not speak but they seemed to understand each other because she turned back to me and said, 'Have you decided to retract your allegation of sexual abuse, Lucy?'

'Yes, absolutely!' I yelled at her, by this time losing control of my emotions. 'I have to do this, don't you understand?' There was a slight pause before Pam gently responded that she did understand very well my fear and the situation that I was placed in.

The tears started to flow down my face now, uncontrollable sobs gripped my entire body. I had my father's life in my hands, yet my own guilty feelings prevented me from deeming him responsible for anything bad that I had experienced at his hands. Harriet passed me a tissue, which I declined to take, preferring to show my independence, and so I used my hands to wipe away my tears. Within a short time I calmed down and the crying ceased. It was important to me not to let my guard down any more than I had done already in front of these too-powerful people who claimed to be on my side whilst they were really there waiting for an opportunity to split my family apart. It was up to me to make sure that this didn't happen. I had to keep the family together.

I asked what would now happen to Daddy. 'Will Daddy be able to stay at home with us now? He won't go to jail or anything will he … please?'

Pam explained to me, 'Your father has already been taken to the police station and interviewed. I'm afraid that he denied that he had sexually abused you so we are unable to prosecute him unless you pursue the charges. Well, unless you make a statement that we can then use to charge your father with.'

'But I don't want to do that. Really I don't.'

Meeting my eyes with her piercing gaze the police lady spoke kindly to me when she said, 'Yes, we understand this, Lucy, and we accept your decision. But it is perfectly normal to be frightened right now. All I can do is to reassure you that should you change your mind then we will be ready to come back and speak to you at any time. Do you understand?'

'Yes, I do understand what you are saying, but that won't be necessary because Daddy didn't do anything bad to me. I lied.' Turning to Harriet, I asked in obvious desperation, 'So, will I still be allowed to go and live back at home now? That is, if my parents ever forgive me for getting Daddy into trouble like this?'

Harriet looked at me with what may have been tears in her eyes, as though she had been here a million times before.

'Yes. I should think that will be possible, when you are discharged from Redfield. But we won't think about this now as that's a long way off yet.'

Thoughts of Daddy's anger were filling my mind with terror and panic. The police lady had told me that Daddy had completely denied ever abusing me. It was what I had expected his reaction to be – after all, he had told me enough times that nobody would believe me anyway, so why would he admit it when he was so sure of that? But still, somewhere deep down inside of me, I knew I had been hoping against all possible hope that Daddy would admit to it. If that had happened, then there might be a chance that Mummy would still be able to love me.

'We won't be charging your father with anything, Lucy,' Pam insisted whilst looking regretfully at me.

'Thank you,' I replied, not really knowing what I was thanking these police officers for.

'We can leave now,' said Harriet.

On hearing these words I rose instantly and walked towards the door. Harriet shook hands with the police lady and then the policeman on her way over to me. I heard her thank them for their time and patience. Then I opened the door and headed out with Harriet following me. To my own surprise I remembered the way out along the corridor, to where the old battered staircase was situated, and I even remembered the way along the white corridors which led out of Jarvis House.

We walked along in silence until we reached the outside of the building. The glaring sunshine took a few seconds to get used to. Harriet looked at me and enquired if I would like to go back to the unit with her. 'We don't expect you to return to school today. You have experienced quite a shock and have been very brave. Why don't we go and get a drink, hey?' After no response from me, Harriet suggested that we get a Coke or an orange.

'I'd really rather go back to classes,' I answered her with determination in my voice. This clearly took Harriet by surprise, so I explained, 'My bag is there … it has all my school books in it and my pencil case…'

'Oh, you really don't need to worry about that, Lucy, I will send Charlotte over to pick it up for you. We'll get your bag back to you in no time.' When I could see that this excuse wasn't going to get me anywhere but back at the unit with all the nurses gaping at me as though I were some prize specimen, I decided just to insist that I wanted to go back to school. 'There's nothing for me to do at the unit as all the other children are at school anyway.'

There was a moment's consideration before Harriet agreed that I could go back into class. She walked me over to the Sea House School unit and took me right into the Home Economics class from which I had earlier been taken away by Charlotte. I was left at my solitary desk after a searching look from Harriet, as if to make sure that I really wanted to be here. There was clearly time in which I could change my mind. Harriet exchanged a few inaudible words with the teacher who smiled nervously in my direction.

As Harriet left the room through the large white double doors I watched her go, feeling great relief that it was all over. Normality had returned. I was sitting here at my school desk. My life was my own again and I could pretend that none of what had just happened had really happened at all. The other girls were still making their marmalade, my French books were lying across the desk exactly as I had left them. The Pooh Bear pencil which Kara had given me for a going away present had remained placed in the same spot beside my books as I had left it. I picked up my blue pencil and looked at the happy picture of Pooh Bear sitting on a patch of grass surrounded by honey pots. He had his paw firmly embedded in one of them, while there were a few solitary bees buzzing around the honey jars. I tried to concentrate hard on this pencil in order to drive away all other thoughts from my mind. I thought that if only I could think of nothing else but Pooh Bear, then nothing bad would happen. All that had just occurred would be undone.

Suddenly, without warning, without even realising that it was about to happen, I collapsed into hysterical sobs. Physically sliding from my chair onto the floor beneath my desk I curled up and let my entire body be taken over by wracking painful sobs. Within seconds Gill, the teacher, had run from the classroom and Harriet had reappeared. She ran over to where I was lying helpless on the cold stone floor and gently knelt beside me. Harriet helped me to my feet while the teacher gathered together the scattered school books and pencil case, placing them all in my blue rucksack.

As I stood up, leaning on Harriet's arm for physical support, the teacher passed my bag to Harriet who took it without a word and put it over her right shoulder. We walked towards the doors, which the teacher held open for Harriet and I to pass through. My entire body felt heavy and I needed to continue holding on to Harriet's arm for physical support. Still crying uncontrollably the entire way, Harriet led me back to Redfield.

Once inside the unit I was led to the dining table and helped to sit down at the table. Harriet sat down at my side. Charlotte brought over a cup of hot sugary tea and I drank this because I was told to. There was no fight left in me, no resistance, I could no longer think. All that I was able to do was to cry without ceasing. Harriet let me do this, ensuring that I drank my tea in between sobs. Her arm was placed around my shoulder but I was unable to take comfort or consolation from this support. For what seemed to me an eternity, I just cried without speaking. The only words that were said to me were 'Drink some tea, there's a good girl', and 'Go on, you cry – let it all out', and so I cried.

When I was forced to stop crying due to the lack of energy

left within my body, I noticed how silent the unit was without the rest of the children. There was literally just myself and the two nurses sat here. Charlotte had since joined us at the table after making the tea. Being the less qualified of the two nurses, Charlotte just seemed to be sitting there watching the whole display of raw emotion that I was pouring out before them.

Several minutes passed in further silence, which I appreciated. There really were no words that could have been uttered to console me at this point. All that could be heard were the faint singing of the birds outside in the fields. I took some deep breaths in order to breathe normally again. Then I wiped my eyes with a paper tissue that had been put before me on the table without my noticing it earlier on in my distress.

I desperately wanted to be alone now, and so I asked the nurses if I could go upstairs to the dorm and have a lie down on my bed. Harriet looked hesitant and explained that the rules were such that during the day we were not allowed to go into the dorms. I knew this already, but I explained how tired I felt. Harriet, being aware of my heart condition, decided that perhaps I really did need to rest after the length of time I had spent crying. I was completely exhausted. But I needed solitude as well right now. Harriet, visibly reluctant, agreed to let me lie down on my bed in the dorm providing Charlotte stayed in the office upstairs all the while I rested. Had it not been for the extenuating circumstance of my heart condition I doubt that I would have been allowed to rest alone at all right then.

Charlotte agreed to sit in the office upstairs while I slept. Slowly I got up from the table and walked past the nurses' office and made my way up the narrow staircase that led to the dorm and bedrooms. My body still felt weak as I walked past the bedrooms and on into the dorm where I slept. As soon as I saw him, I grabbed hold of Pooh Bear and held him close to my chest. 'You're my only friend in the whole world,' I whispered to him, with a few tears rolling down my face only to land on the top of bear's furry faded yellow head. I threw myself face down on the top of my bed covers with Pooh Bear beneath me. I put my right thumb in my mouth as I usually did when I went to sleep or when I felt in need of comfort.

For a long while I just lay there, thinking about the day's events and how everything had seemed so much better yesterday. I wondered if I would ever be forgiven by Mummy or if she would really hate me forever like Daddy had told me would happen if she ever found out about this stuff. I reasoned that I had denied it, so surely Mummy couldn't hate me for doing it with Daddy because she still wouldn't know. Then Kara somehow made her way into my thoughts. She needed me more than she would ever realise. For Kara's sake I had to go back home, to look out for her. It was the least I could do for my own sister. I just hoped that I would be allowed to go back home soon and that my parents would accept me back again. Daddy had warned me recently that if I tried to resist him when he touched me then he would have to go in to my sister's room and hurt Kara instead. He gave me a choice to protect my sister.

For at least an hour or so I must have fallen into a deep sleep. The physical exhaustion of my body finally overcame the intrusive thoughts, which were dominating my mind. The very next thing that I remembered was Rebecca in her long black gothic style dress, standing over me trying to rouse me by shaking me. 'It's dinner time, Lucy. Wakey wakey. Lucy …' hearing my name being spoken in Rebecca's shrill voice roused me from my surprisingly peaceful slumber.

'Dinner … Rebecca? It's you? … Where am I?'

Rebecca giggled before reminding me that I was in Redfield – asleep – at dinner time. She emphasised the word 'asleep' as though it were unbelievable that someone could sleep through dinner. 'Adam sent me up to wake you. Charlotte's gone downstairs to the office just now as they're handing over onto the nightshift. You've got about five minutes before dinner will be served – come on,' insisted Rebecca, tugging at my arm while she spoke. 'Get up, lazy bones!'

'OK, OK, I'm coming,' I replied.

'Adam is on duty with Christina tonight,' Rebecca further informed me, knowing I would be pleased that Adam was on duty. He often played pool with me and spent time just with me before bed, chatting about this and that. He seemed to want to get to know me as a person, like he actually cared or something.

Without wanting to, I left Pooh Bear behind on my bed, after tucking him into the covers so that he would be safe and warm for when I returned to bed a few hours later. Following Rebecca down the narrow staircase, her mindless chatter about nothing in particular served to distract my attention from what had happened to me earlier in the day. As I explained to you before, it was a rule of thumb that no one in this place pried into anyone else's business. We each had our own problems to deal with and it was our choice if we spoke about them to each other. Rebecca was no doubt curious as to why I had left school twice in the same day, but to ask would have been to defy all show of respect for each other's private pain.

'Do you want to play pool tonight, Lucy? ... I was just thinking that we could rope Christina into playing Monopoly with us if you'd like to thrash Adam!'

Understanding Rebecca's kind intentions behind this, I thanked her and said that would be good. 'I don't really feel like being crowded tonight Rebecca, I guess that time alone with Adam might just about be bearable ... Thanks.'

'No problem – any time, really. The others won't mind either, you know that.'

Having said this we walked together past the nurses' office and took our places at the dining table. I did feel as though everyone's eyes were on me, probably because they were. No one confronted me, as I had expected would be the case. But still they were thinking about what could be going on, and just that knowledge in itself made me feel conspicuous.

Dinner was brought over to the table – nothing special, just a chicken pie and soggy mashed potatoes with the token vegetables of peas and carrots. Just looking at the dish placed before me made me feel sick, let alone actually tasting it. I played around with the potatoes on my plate for a bit before Christina asked me if I would like to leave my meal. I said yes, and went to place my plate on the metal meal trolley, which was always left in the kitchen. After meals the porter on duty would come and remove the trolley.

Christina offered me pudding, but I firmly declined any ice cream. I just couldn't face eating, I had lost my appetite completely – even for ice cream. In light of this I asked for permission to leave the table and to go over and sit in one of the more comfy chairs over by the pool table. Christina agreed instantly. I glanced at Adam who looked back at me tenderly as I left the table.

I sat myself down and picked up some magazine from the little coffee table next to the chair. It was intended for teenagers, so I leafed through it trying to read the articles on 'How to Kiss' and all that sort of thing. I could hear and see the others eating their meal at the table. Their chatter was inane and unremarkable – pretty much like the contents of the magazine that I was flicking through. It was not too long before Adam came over to where I was seated and invited me to play pool with him. I agreed to a game, knowing that he was just trying to show me some moral support. After all, even if Adam won the game of pool, as was usually the case, what more was left of any importance in my life that I could possibly lose today?

Chapter 6

After the pool game ended – which I well and truly lost to Adam who, as always, was the reigning champion – I gratefully clambered into bed. Still exhausted and in shock from the day's events, I fell into a remarkably deep sleep that night from which no dark demon of terror managed to drag me. Sleep is supposedly the body's natural means to recovery, so maybe that's the reason why I was able to sleep peacefully and undisturbed. Not even Elaine called on me throughout that night, although she probably did need my help, but saw that my need for sleep was greater than her need for my assistance at that time. That's what friends are for, I guess.

Elaine is the first real friend that I have ever had, really. She is the first person who has ever really spent much time with me and actually listened to what I have to say. Of course that works both ways, but we kind of just get on, if that makes any sense. We seem to understand so much about each other without even speaking. Almost as though words are not even necessary to communicate all that we have to relate to each other. Elaine is much quieter than I am, though. She keeps a lot inside her, bottled up. A lot of personal stuff, I mean. Having been through several foster homes I would imagine that she has many stories she could tell, if only she were able to find the words with which to convey them. Apparently each of her foster parents have rejected her on various grounds. The main reason seems to be because she wets the bed frequently at night-time. Elaine told me once that she always feels as though she is on trial for the first few weeks that she is placed in a new foster home.

The various foster parents who have taken Elaine into their homes have differed in their treatment of her – that's about all I know, as Elaine does not talk much about her experiences. But she did tell me that each family she has ever been placed with has expected her to quit the bed-wetting once she has had what they have deemed to be sufficient time to settle in. When this has not been the case they have invariably returned her to the social service department. Elaine has changed school so many times that she said to me she has lost count. At least I have only been to one grammar school.

At Harrington High School I was kind of ostracised on the grounds that I was fairly boring. Seriously, due to the fact that I was forbidden to participate in games or physical education as a safeguard against my heart condition deteriorating, I was unable to be included in any form of activity that might be designed to unite children in mutual friendship. There were no common interests that I could find with the other children. Apart from reading books and sitting quietly in the corner while the other children were outside in the play-ground, getting to know each other, there was not much else that I could do at school. No matter what the weather was like, I was never allowed to step outside into the playground. This remained the case throughout both primary school and grammar school. Having said this, it is undoubtedly the reason why I perform exceptionally well in academic terms. There is nothing else at school for me to concentrate on so I tend to focus on those subjects that I really enjoy, like English and art history, and hence I do well in terms of grades.

To be fair, though, I was allowed to miss class whenever I felt like it. Technically I was only meant to leave the classroom and attend the sickbay when I felt tired or unwell. The sickbay at Harrington High School is situated right at the end of a long corridor in the basement of the English department building. There is a nurse on constant duty and a rusty old bed in the corner of the nurse's tiny office where I was expected to lay down and sleep or read quietly to myself.

I was always allowed to rest whenever I felt that I needed to. I knew that I could just leave my desk and absent myself from the class without any questions being asked. I suspect now that the teachers may have known that I was using this to my advantage at times, but declined to say anything perhaps on the grounds that if I had been truly unwell then they would have been held accountable. Children are aware of their power in such situations.

However, maths classes always used to make me feel incredibly tired for some unknown reason, so I tended to fall ill an awful lot during those lessons. Mr Martin was a tall hairy bearded man who had the most dreadful bad breath. It was a problem, because maths was difficult enough to understand without having to hold your breath while he leant across your desk explaining Pythagorean theory to you for the fifth time during that lesson. Maths was the only subject that I never managed to achieve an A grade in. I was lucky if I even managed a C on most exercises.

I would sit at my desk completely bewildered by this world of numbers and signs and algebraic equations that were displayed before me on the blackboard. No matter how hard I tried, I could never see the logic behind any of it. So I would often yawn for a bit, then quietly rise from my desk and gather together my school bag and leave the class. Mr Martin would glance sympathetically at me as though he believed that I was really ill.

The other children in my classes tended not to take any notice of me at all. They could not understand why so many concessions were made for me as was frequently demonstrated by their thoughtless remarks such as, 'You're so lucky that you don't have to do physical education ... we hate it ... it's not fair...' If only they could have understood that I would have exchanged all of my so-called privileges in a second if it had been possible for me to have lived a more normal life, such as the lives that I saw them living. Even if I did have to return to Harrington High it won't really make a great deal of difference either way. I didn't have any friends there before I came to Redfield so I wasn't likely to have any when or if I had to go back to that school.

Of course there were times when I did genuinely feel the need to rest. Having two holes in my heart and a damaged lung does place quite a demand on one's body to keep up with the rest of the world. Three major open-heart surgery operations have left me with an extremely tender scar, right down the middle of my chest cavity. It is a very neat line in point of fact as my heart surgeon Professor Jacobs is the best in the world. He has done a wonderful job on me and this is reflected by the fact that I am neatly sewn up. There are some doctors of course who refuse to accept that this dead tissue which forms the scar is sensitive to the touch of their stethoscope. Inevitably they place that ghastly piece of metal too near the scar so that I have to jump away from them or literally push their stethoscope away from my too-sore flesh. This makes consultations difficult at the very least. My own GP, Dr Sebastian Taylor, is dreadfully unsympathetic to my plight in this respect. I suspect that he deliberately places his stethoscope over the sensitive scar tissue area because he knows it causes me unbearable discomfort.

The worst operation that I had to undergo was when I was seven and a half years old. This took place at the hospital that I still regularly attend in London. After an eight-and-a-half-hour operation, which is the longest heart and lung operation that I have yet had to undergo, the surgeon left the stitches in me so that they had to be removed after the surgery – with me fully conscious, as opposed to dissolvable stitches. I had to be held down by three nurses while those damn stitches were removed. I think that I screamed so loudly that the entire city of London must have heard me!

There was a slightly older boy called James in the bed opposite to mine who also had to have his stitches removed on the same day. James and I, with no little encouragement from our parents, made a bet that entailed behaving admirably throughout the entire stitches removal. The deal was made that whoever behaved the best would get a present. His father along with my mother bought each of us presents before this dreadful ordeal was about to take place. James had asked my mother to buy him loads of salt and vinegar crisps – that was all he had wanted – so James's father bought me some chocolates as that had been my request. The idea initially had been that we were meant to consume our present *after* the removal of the stitches. Yet James apparently ate the entire twenty packets of crisps that my mother had bought him throughout the procedure of his stitches removal! He didn't make so much as a squeak, whereas the whole ward heard me and my vociferous futile protests throughout the entire horrible experience!

I was lying on my bed listening to my mother's soft voice reading to me the story about Pooh Sticks when, surrounded by three undoubtedly adoring nurses, the doctor in his long swishing white coat began his walk along the brightly coloured children's ward towards my bed. Cheerful Sparrows ward is a small, intimate ward for very sick children, all of whom suffer with heart and lung conditions. This is an internationally renowned specialist hospital devoted to treating just heart and lung disease.

It is also a training hospital where junior doctors attend the ward rounds with the heart specialists. The appearance of several – usually male – doctors hovering over my bed, each examining me in turn, always unnerved me. Particularly as the consultant cardiologist would often shout at these equally nervous doctors and I would be left wondering if it were my fault that they were being told off. However, on noticing the arrival of the doctor, I tried to concentrate hard upon the moment when Eeyore fell into the water as a result of being bounced by Tigger. I considered it possible that if I just thought about Eeyore and Tigger and Mummy reading to me then the doctor may not notice that I was there and hence he might just go away. Obviously this did not happen, in spite of my deperate hopes that it would.

The doctor approached my bed within moments of his arrival in the ward. The helpful nurses began to draw the curtains around me, simultaneously telling my mother that the doctor was ready to examine my stitches before removal. Immediately, I started to resist, knowing from the outset that this was going to be no picnic. My chest was already extremely tender, sore and red from its recent reopening. I did not want anyone near it, let alone pulling the stitches out one by one. They were deeply embedded within my painful wound, knotted at the outside, which no doubt caused further discomfort and contributed to my lack of mobility.

'Come along, Lucy, there's a good girl, let the doctor take a look at you ...' Mummy instantly held my left hand down, while a nurse managed to hold my right hand down by standing alongside of the opposite side of my bed. I wriggled and writhed about for some moments trying to get free from this restraint, but it was of no use. The doctor sat down beside me and told me to keep still and relax as he was only going to take a look for the time being. I lay very still and held my breath while he looked closely at the gash along my chest. Then he started to feel the stitches, at which point I screamed with all the strength I had inside my tiny body.

I vaguely remember the cutting of the knots, then the slight tugging at the stitch as it was pulled out of its place. The heart monitor that I was attached to started beeping erratically as my heart raced with fear and my body writhed beneath this agonising pain. The third nurse was asked to hold my legs still as I had begun to kick them violently in the air in an attempt to free myself. I was finally unable to move and the doctor was able to remove the twelve stitches one by one without any movement from my now helpless body. The only option left open to me was to scream out my pain in the hope that someone from outside the curtains would come to my rescue, to relieve me from this unbearable torture and send the nasty doctor away. When this did not happen I tried to escape into the curtain itself through my mind. I switched off from the physical pain that was being executed upon my conscious form, while I tried to put myself into the trees that were depicted on the light green curtains around my bed. All the time, the screaming continued aloud yet, given the total lack of response, they may as well have been silent screams.

This tactic of escape was going to be needed again many times throughout my life, particularly when I returned back home. Only then the screaming would become as silent and immobile as this body while my mind drifted elsewhere in an effort to escape from the otherwise intolerable pain and fear. Often when Daddy hurt me in my bed at night, I looked up at the ceiling in an effort to displace myself into the vast space above me. Rather than concentrate on Daddy's heavy breathing I tried to disconnect myself from the situation. Almost as though not thinking about it at the time would make it unreal.

The heart problems seem like such a long time ago now. For two years I have not had to be reopened for surgery as my heart has managed to maintain a steady working rhythm with the help of a pacemaker. This mechanical object was fitted when I was just eleven years old. It works by sensing the electrical activity in my heart. There are two wires fitted which connect the pacemaker to my heart and they send electrical signals back to my heart in order to kick-start it when it begins to slow down. The cardiologist said that I suffer from 'heart failure', but that it is not as serious as it sounds! It simply means that my little heart is unable to function as well as it ought to at my age. That's why I have never been allowed to do anything too strenuous.

Professor Summers explained that my heart had already done the work of a sixty-year-old woman at the age of eleven, so rather than be disappointed in having a weak heart I ought to be proud of its strength to continue in light of its difficulties. Perhaps there is consolation to be found in this fact.

I guess that there are not many sixty-year-old women who would enjoy the light game of badminton that I am now allowed to participate in, or even be able to go ice-skating! There are some good things about being here in Redfield. If I were still at school, these activities would certainly be disallowed.

But that was then. Now I had to face a far bigger problem in terms of fighting to regain my family's love and acceptance, as opposed to fighting for my life. Although the two issues may not be as mutually exclusive as they appear to be. Somehow I made it through the following week. Harriet informed me the morning after the dreadful police interview that my mother was coming to see me on the forthcoming Saturday. I was on edge for the entire three days preceding this visit from my mother.

This wasn't helped by the fact that I succumbed to a full-blown asthma attack on the Wednesday evening. Elaine, Siobhan and I were playing Cluedo when I first started to become wheezy. We were sitting around the dining table, engrossed in our game when Professor Plum – myself – was revealed as the murderer. I had stabbed Miss Scarlet in the library. Upon this revelation my wheezing turned into a restriction across my chest cavity at which point breathing became increasingly difficult. Breathing out was the most uncomfortable. I didn't panic initially, because I knew that that would be the worse thing to do in the circumstances.

Having experienced many asthma attacks I knew that panicking only served to exacerbate my already poor breathing ability.

Fortunately Siobhan had her wits about her and ran to inform the nurses in the office immediately. Christina called an ambulance while Adam came over to me with my inhalers. I tried to take in Ventolin but it was virtually impossible. The restriction in my airways meant that the inhaler was ineffective. Adam held my hand and told me to remain calm and to breathe slowly. I was aware that over-breathing only leads to a too-high intake of carbon dioxide. Within a short while the ambulance arrived. I had sufficient time to notice the fright on the faces of Siobhan and Elaine. Rebecca by now had also left the television to come and watch the real-life drama unfold before her disbelieving eyes.

Immediately upon their arrival the ambulance crew fitted me with an oxygen mask and then felt my pulse. I was taken out into the ambulance in a wheelchair, as lying down would have worsened the asthma attack. The oxygen mask brought small relief. Adam, as the more senior nurse, remained behind at Redfield while Christina came with me in the ambulance. As soon as I was wheeled outside of the unit, I felt the cold blast of air engulf my body and momentarily stop my breathing. The ambulance crew hurriedly fixed me securely inside the big white ambulance. The smell of death seemed to linger in the air and I looked at the black leather narrow bed opposite me, wondering how many deaths had taken place right there, in front of this very same crew.

For the first time in my entire life I was taken into a general medical hospital without my mother present. I was used to my father being absent from the hospital when I was ill, but my mother had always been with me. This time I was stuck with a psychiatric nurse from Redfield who refused to leave me and, more importantly, to call my mother. Despairing and distraught, the asthma attack worsened until I was placed inside an oxygen tent and admitted to the hospital for the entire night.

The oxygen tent was fitted around my bed in the children's ward. There were a few babies crying when I arrived on the trolley. The ward was in darkness except for a few odd lamps, which were left on above some of the beds. There was also the familiar sound of the heart monitors beeping quietly and regularly, which reminded me as soon as I awoke in the morning that I was in hospital. My breathing settled down to a fairly steady rhythm after about an hour inside the oxygen tent, but the decision was made to leave me inside the tent throughout the rest of the night. Sleep soon took over, even before Christina left my bedside. Although Mummy was not there I went to sleep with the hope that she would be when I woke up in the morning. However this was not to be the case.

A doctor visited in the morning and pronounced me fit and well. After examining my heart and lungs for what felt like an hour, he said that there didn't seem to be any further problems now that the asthma attack had subsided. A short course of prednisolene steroid tablets was prescribed to safeguard against the airways in my lungs becoming restricted again in the near future.

I ate a lonely breakfast of Cornflakes with dry toast and then took a shower. The hospital nurses were fully aware that I was from Redfield and hence they watched me like a hawk – there was no real chance that I could have escaped anyway, given my weakened condition.

Whilst in the middle of a game of Jackstraws with a smart nine-year-old called Rick, Harriet arrived to collect me. I was disappointed that my mother never showed up. It was the first time that I had been in a hospital without her support and comfort. On noticing Harriet, I put on my brave face and acted as though I didn't have a care in the world.

Harriet spoke briefly to the sister in charge and then

greeted me. 'I hear that you've been having some fun and games, kid!' she chuckled. 'Are you ready to leave?'

With a smile I acknowledged that I was indeed ready to leave. As I had been rushed in to the ward during the night I didn't have any belongings to take with me. I had worn a hospital gown throughout the night so I was dressed in the same clothes which I came in with. It hadn't occurred to Harriet to bring any fresh clothes along to the hospital. My mother would not have forgotten to do that.

In the ride back to the unit, which was in the official white bus, Harriet and I hardly spoke to each other after it was ascertained that Mummy had indeed been informed of my asthma attack the night before, but had decided not to come to the hospital. Apparently she had said that as she knew I was being taken care of there was 'no need' for her to rush all the way over to Canterbury. My heart sank to the very depths of my being, certain in the knowledge that my own mother hated me and wished that I were dead. Clearly I was not about to be forgiven. As for my father, I was pretty sure that if he got his hands on me then he would kill me himself.

All I knew for certain was that Mummy would be coming here at around 10 a.m. on the forthcoming Saturday morning – without my father. He was refusing to speak to me.

When we arrived back at the unit, Elaine, Rebecca and Siobhan were already in school as it was nearly 11.30 a.m. Apparently the ward sister had told Harriet that the best place for me that day would be in bed. As a result I was expected to go upstairs to my dorm and get straight back into bed again. I protested on the grounds that I really was not feeling tired enough to go to bed.

'But at least you will be resting and that's just as important as sleeping.' Having said this, I was sent up to my bed. Harriet sat in the nurses' office near the dorm while I read a book in bed and drifted in and out of sleep.

After school was finished, Elaine was given special

permission to sit with me on my bed and I was thankful for this opportunity to have some decent company. We talked about the night before and how exciting and scary it had all been for the other girls, seeing me hardly able to breathe. I told Elaine that I wasn't scared at all, not for a second, although in all honesty I was probably the one who had been the most afraid.

Elaine was wearing a pair of faded blue jeans that were clearly a size too big for her, and a baggy red sweatshirt. She looked somewhat lonely and despondent, so when I realised that something was seriously troubling her I asked if she would tell me what was on her mind. After a moment's hesitation she decided that she would speak to me about what was upsetting her, on the strict understanding that I would not discuss it with anybody else. I agreed to this rule with no intention of betraying her confidence. Although talking to you does not really count because she will never know about this stuff, right?

Elaine, who never found it easy to talk about herself a great deal at the best of times, began to tell me she had received news just that morning, before school, that a new foster family had been found for her. 'I have to go and spend the weekend with them this Saturday,' she quietly informed me. 'Just like that ... I haven't even had a chance to meet them or anything.' I listened, not knowing what to say. 'I'm more afraid of liking them than disliking them. Every time I like a family that I am with, they decide that they don't want me any more because of ... you know ...' I quickly acknowledged that I knew what she was referring to, in order to save Elaine from undue embarrassment, and she continued by asking, 'What is the point of me even going there when they won't want me anyway?'

She quit talking for a while and I sat beside her on my bed, not quite knowing what to say that would console her. I thought that it was cruel of the nurses and social services to get her hopes up, only for them to be repeatedly dashed. But I did not say this aloud, as I felt that it would serve no constructive purpose.

Elaine looked at me with those deep sorrowful eyes, almost filled with tears. 'This will be the seventh foster home that I've had to go into, Lucy. It's not nice being in foster care. Anything's got to be better than this.'

Without realising what she had said, Elaine had set off within me a train of thought which led to exactly the same conclusion. At least I had always had a secure, stable home up until now. It was my own fault that my home life was in such serious jeopardy at the moment. In spite of the bad stuff Daddy did to me, he did a lot of good things for all of us too, like buying our clothes and toys, and sometimes taking us to the park. And anyway, the bad stuff was my fault because I made him so angry with me all the time. He told me that if only I was a good girl, then he would not have to hurt me.

'I wish we could run away and be together forever. Just us.' I agreed that it would be a cool thing to do, but virtually impossible to achieve in light of all the security surrounding this place. Elaine confided in me that she had saved a lot of money from her weekly allowance and had it stashed at the back of one of her shoes. 'Perhaps we could use that,' she joked.

'It wouldn't get us very far, Elaine. Even if we did manage to escape from Redfield, they would find us eventually. You know that too, don't you?'

Pausing, she reluctantly admitted to holding the same conviction.

'What do you know about these prospective foster parents? Have the nurses told you anything?' I enquired.

'Well, it was my social worker, Mrs Phillips, who came to see me this morning before school. She told me that the couple are professional people – well, that he is, anyway. Apparently he is a bank manager. But his wife doesn't do anything except foster kids. They have two others already, but they are both a lot younger than me. I think Mrs Phillips said that the boy Jack is ten, and the girl Amanda is four.'

Elaine and I exchanged knowing glances, well aware from previous conversations that if she were not found a permanent foster home by the age of sixteen then she would be put into some grotty little bedsit by the local social services department.

'This might be my last hope, Lucy. I will be sixteen in less than two years' time … I want … I need a family … I have no one … No one wants to foster or adopt someone of my age, Lucy.'

I put my arm round her shoulder. 'You will always have me, Elaine. I will always be your friend, I promise, no matter what.'

Half of me was afraid of ending up in the same situation as Elaine. For all intents and purposes I too had lost my family, and at a time when I most needed their support. But worst of all, I knew that I had only myself to blame. Elaine could hardly be held responsible for her current predicament.

We just hugged each other in silence for a short while until Elaine spoke. 'Are your parents still coming to see you this Saturday?' she asked me timidly, unsure as to whether or not she was speaking out of line.

'Mummy is, but as far as I know Daddy can't make it this week.' I couldn't face telling Elaine the whole truth.

'So, Saturday it is then,' said Elaine with her despair barely concealed as she uttered the words.

'Yep, Saturday it is,' I agreed.

Chapter 7

Saturday morning arrived all too soon, as I waited with bated breath for Mummy to walk through the doors at Redfield. I really had no idea what to expect from her. She may have been coming to tell me that she no longer wanted anything to do with me, she may have been coming to tell me that she would never forgive me for the things that I have done with Daddy. I was unsure as to what to prepare for. But rejection was a sure thing.

Anxiety prevented me from being able to eat any breakfast. My stomach felt as though it were in knots and the rest of me felt as though I were splintered into a million different pieces.

While the other girls sat down to breakfast I asked to be excused and went and sat in the sitting area, alone. I took advantage of the opportunity that solitude allowed, to play my own choice of music without interruption or complaint from any of the others. I knew that music would be the only thing that stood a chance of being able to distract my attention from what lay ahead today.

I placed Bon Jovi's CD *Cross Road* into the stereo and selected my favourite track, *Someday I'll Be Saturday Night*. Although it was already Saturday today as I well knew, I always carried the hope inside of me that I personally would one day reach the Saturday night which Jon Bon Jovi was singing about.

Bon Jovi had been my favourite band for over a year now. I had really only got into pop music because I heard one of their songs on the radio when I was in the car with Daddy. He was driving me to a piano lesson at the time but I was so afraid of making him cross during the journey that I focused my attention really hard on the radio in an attempt to make Daddy's physical presence go away from my mind.

To try to manage the fear of Daddy being angry I concentrated really hard on the music which was being played. Coincidentally the track being played was *Runaway* by Bon Jovi. After the song was finished the DJ explained that it was the first song that Jon Bon Jovi had ever written and released and that it was an instant success. The lyrics really spoke to me and reflected my own desire to run away from home and my life.

Because I had been so impressed with this song and the power of excellent musicians to reflect one's inner self and enable one to express one's soul in a safe but nonetheless strong form, I decided to use my pocket money to buy Bon Jovi's latest CD, *Cross Road*.

As soon as I heard *Someday I'll Be Saturday Night* I knew that it was written for me. I mean; not literally – but really if Bon Jovi had needed a model for that song I could have been it. *Someday I'll Be Saturday Night* gave me the hope that there really could be another day, another way to live one's life. That the dice can fall in any number of ways. I hope that one day I really will make it to Saturday night, that I won't get stuck on Wednesday.

Wednesday is, ironically, the one day that is not referred to by name in the lyrics. Perhaps because that kind of pain – the type of pain and suffering that one is born into – is beyond all redemption. Possibly Wednesday's child can never know what it is to experience any other kind of day. Perhaps no effort, no hard work, no determination or fearlessness and courage in the face of great danger will ever mean anything to a Wednesday's child. Maybe dice are designed always to be loaded against a Wednesday's child.

However, I am with Bon Jovi on this and I do choose to believe that someday I will be that Saturday night, that I will make it to the day when I can be free and have choices regarding how to live my own life. It is enough just to hope that I will eventually gain the freedom to be allowed to have my own life. Each time that I listen to *Someday I'll Be Saturday Night* I am inspired by the earnestness of the lyrics which were so artfully penned by Jon Bon Jovi, Richie Sambora and Desmond Child. I am encouraged and convinced to decide that no dice or challenges or cruel parents will make me stay behind on a Wednesday when Saturday is just three days away.

The *Cross Road* album itself is an excellent compilation of their hits, including *Runaway. Keep The Faith* is another track which I play to help me to hold on when things are getting a little too tough and Thursday is beginning to look as though it may never arrive, let alone the promised Saturday!

At home I spend many hours after school and at weekends just lying on my bed with my toys and our golden Labrador Frazier, just listening to Bon Jovi repeatedly. My dog, my toys and I also admire the many posters of Bon Jovi which cover every inch of available wall space in my bedroom. I always have the stereo blasting out Bon Jovi songs as loudly as I am allowed to get away with. My parents dislike them which is pretty neat too!

In order to focus my mind and ease the unbearable anxiety which I was feeling I tried to concentrate on Jon Bon Jovi's voice. He started to sing *Someday* when Elaine walked into the sitting area. His powerful vocals were beginning to distract me from the impending visit.

'What are you listening to?' Elaine asked, genuinely not having heard of Bon Jovi before.

'Bon Jovi,' I answered with the only smile that I had managed all morning.

'Oh, they are beginning to grow on me now. I hear you playing this album a lot. I just never knew who they were.' She offered almost apologetically. Before arriving to stay at Redfield Elaine had never had a permanent bedroom or home. That's why she did not have any posters to look at or pop music to play. It was not her fault that she did not know anything about the wonderful Bon Jovi. At least she had me to introduce her to all their work!

We both sat there listening to the CD until Siobhan waltzed into the sitting area and immediately switched the stereo off. She said she was suffering with a headache and needed some peace and quiet. Not wanting to question this or face a confrontation Elaine and I decided to ask for permission to take a walk outside. Elaine went off to ask the nearest available nurse while I headed over to the door in hopeful anticipation of being allowed to go outside.

My spirits felt lifted a little since listening to Bon Jovi. They reminded me of all that was good in the world; they stood for all that was worth living for. One day I will meet them, I told myself. One day they will know what they got me through.

With permission duly granted Elaine and I walked out into the designated garden area around the Redfield unit. The reason that we were given extra privileges like this again was based on the fact that we had proved ourselves to be trustworthy and unlikely to run away or cause any damage – towards ourselves or towards each other. She was as anxious as I was to get through today, but for different reasons. Today really was make or break time for both of us. Elaine told me that she had all her hopes in this new foster placement working out, as it would not be likely that Mrs Phillips, her social worker, would be able to continue finding any more families willing to take her on if this seventh attempt failed also. We sat down on the lawn and just watched the blades of grass swaying to and fro within the gentle breeze.

'Man is but a reed, but he is a thinking reed' – I quoted Pascal to Elaine, thinking that it would put a smile on her face, and it worked. She started to playfight with me and so we ended up tumbling around all over these 'thinking reeds' of blades of grass.

I was pinned down begging for mercy for being a thinking reed when Will ventured out into the field and asked if Elaine would like to go with him in to the office.

'Have *they* arrived?' Elaine tentatively enquired. Will nodded. Elaine slowly stood up and simultaneously released my pinned-down wrists from her grip. She brushed down her green tartan skirt and white shirt so that she would look more respectable and tidy. Will waited for her near the door. This gave me an opportunity to discreetly hug Elaine and wish her good luck for the weekend.

'I hope it works out well for you Elaine, but if not, I'll be here when you get back anyway.'

She wiped a tear away from her large dark eyes and walked over to meet Will and her prospective parents. My heart ached for Elaine as I considered the setbacks that she had already had to face.

I didn't manage to catch sight of Elaine's new foster parents as I stayed on in the garden for a short while. Eventually the nurses who were on day duty for the weekend, Kate and Will, both came out to me and asked to speak with me in the office. I followed them into their big room with the glass window overlooking the entire open floor of Redfield. I declined to sit down, as I felt too anxious to rest easy in a chair. It was nearly 10 a.m. and so I was acutely conscious of the fact that Mummy was due to arrive at any moment.

Kate, who could only have been in her mid-twenties, asked me if I would like either herself or Will to sit in with me in the interview room, which is located next to the nurses' office, when my mother arrived to see me. Kate's shoulder-length ginger hair always looked really shiny, especially against the green dress that she often wore and I found myself wondering how she managed to get her hair to look that way, when Will repeated the question. I was easily distracted from the task in hand when I was under severe pressure or mental strain, as the nurses evidently realised by now.

'Erm no ... it's really unnecessary. In fact it would be easier for me if I could be left alone with my mother.'

The nurses looked at each other before Will, who was the more senior nurse, spoke. 'It may be easier for you if you had some moral support, kid. Are you sure you want to be alone?' Will is a kind man, about fifty. He dresses like an elderly man with his jumpers and corduroy trousers and all that, but he always speaks kindly and softly so I guess that makes him OK. Although, don't misunderstand me, I wouldn't want to be left alone with any man in this place. I really wouldn't trust any of them not to hurt me. They all wear belts. Just seeing so much as a glimpse of a black leather belt around a man's waist is enough to instil fear in me.

My stomach felt knotted along with the tension throughout my entire body. I wanted today to be over more than I had wanted anything else in the world. I had dressed well today, wearing my favourite pink dress with the frills and the bows at each side of the dress. In my hair I wore a matching light pink ribbon. I knew that both my parents liked this dress on me, so I wore it with the intention of proving to my mother that I am still the same person that she had loved before.

As Will was about to lead me out of the office, my mother walked into the unit chaperoned on either side, unexpectedly, by my maternal grandparents. We all three caught each other unawares. For a moment I took in the deep sadness that was hardly concealed by their eyes when they each looked at me, and I at them in turn. My grandparents are in their sixties, and at that moment every year of their lives seemed to show in lines embedded across their faces.

Grandpa wore a dark grey cardigan with matching trousers and brown leather Hush Puppy shoes. His silvery grey hair was thinning even more on top than it had been before I was admitted to Redfield, and he had it brushed across his head as though he were trying to cover up the slight baldness that was beginning to make itself visible. He cast down his tearful brown eyes as soon as he met my glance. Grandpa frequently did this, as though he were afraid that if he allowed anyone to look too deeply into his eyes then they would see too much. He looked as though he were in a great deal of pain.

My grandma stood to the left side of my mother, her somewhat large frame overshadowing Mummy's tiny body. She wore a white chiffon blouse with a navy blue skirt covered in tiny white flowery shapes. Around her neck was her favourite blue chiffon scarf, pinned together with the imitation gold butterfly brooch which I had given her for Christmas last year. Her dark brown hair was beginning to show shocking streaks of grey at the sides of her head, above her ears. The grey stood out all the more against the dark brown hair. Grandma's face was more wrinkled with old age than I had ever remembered it to be. As we made eye contact, Grandma looked at me with a penetrating searching gaze that momentarily rooted me to the spot.

As for Mummy and I, we were barely able to look at each other. Shame filled me as I stood before my family, my secret revealed yet retracted. Spoken yet silenced. Mummy wore a light brown summer dress with brown strappy leather sandals. I noticed her open-toed sandals and the pearl nail polish that she was wearing on her toes. She struck me as being more fragile and dainty than I had ever before known her to be.

Of course I knew that in our household Daddy made all the rules and that Mummy never questioned his authority on anything. I guess that's because she loves him so much. After all, he treats her really well and takes care of all of us. Mummy is not even allowed to go out to work for herself because Daddy said that no wife of his has to earn her own money. That's how much he cares for Mummy. I guess that she is really lucky to be married to Daddy from her point of view, because he is so good to her and all. She just sits around and reads or paints watercolours all day without a care in the world. The only time she has ever had to worry has been when I get sick. That's such a hassle because then we have to travel all the way up to London to the hospital for treatment and usually Mummy has to stay alone in a hotel room all the while that I am kept in hospital. I know for a fact that she feels scared when she has to stay alone like that, because she has told me on countless occasions that she feels afraid.

Daddy never comes to the London hospital when I have to be admitted, because he is so busy with working for the local council and all that sort of thing. The nature of his work is such that he can't just leave it for weeks on end and wait around in London for me to recover from heart surgery. So Mummy and I are always left alone. It's kind of good in a way because it is the only time that I ever get Mummy all to myself. I mean without Kara and Anthony demanding her time as well.

She's always real nice to me when I am in hospital, except that she doesn't hug me much like I see the other kids' mothers doing to them. But that's just the way she is – Mummy isn't a physical type of person, it's just not in her nature to be so. After a blood test, for example, she just says 'There there', and expects me to suddenly stop crying and be OK even though it hurts like hell. Needles breaking my skin tend to make me cry. But then Daddy makes me cry more than that and I sure as hell don't get any comfort from anyone then either. Mummy doesn't know about that stuff so it's hardly her fault that I am left to suffer alone.

Will saw that nobody was about to speak or move first, so he ushered us all into the tiny office which is next door to the nurses' larger office where I had just been asked if I required their 'support' during Mummy's visit. Will looked with great compassion at my mother and then at my grandparents as they took the seats that were offered to them. The seats were quite low down and I felt more in control of the situation and of myself if I remained standing. My grandpa must have felt the same way because he stood up almost as soon as he had sat down. The room was square and quite airless so Grandpa went and stood by the window that was closed. He didn't try to open it, probably thinking that the windows in here were not able to open at all in case one of us girls tried to escape through it.

I remained standing directly opposite Grandpa. I was right beside the door so that at literally any moment I could escape from their presence. Mummy and Grandma remained seated opposite each other. There was a small open space in between us where Will had been standing all this time. He offered tea or coffee but everyone declined. Mummy just shook her head as though she no longer had the strength left to even speak.

At this point Will decided to leave us to it. 'If you need me then I'll be next door.' Turning to me, he stated emphatically, 'You know where I am, Lucy.' As he left the room he went to pull the door closed behind him but I stopped him from doing this. I left the door slightly ajar so that I could breathe. The air was stuffy and hot and I really felt as though I were about to suffocate just standing there.

For a few minutes nobody spoke to each other. We all just remained in our positions like statues, without life or blood coursing through our veins. My eyes were fixed firmly on the floor, not knowing what to do or say to these three people whom I loved more than anything else in the world, yet having to live with the knowledge that I had hurt these people more than anyone else could ever do.

Mummy spoke first. She looked up directly in my direction and I felt her eyes burning me with hatred as she asked – as she demanded to know – 'Is it true? Is it true then? Tell me is it true?' The hysteria in her voice was undeniable. The tears poured down her face as she screamed at me uncontrollably, demanding that I tell her if *it* were true or not.

I looked at her in amazement. For a few seconds I really thought that she was asking me. For a brief moment in time I believed that my mother genuinely wanted to know if Daddy had hurt me. It seemed as though she did want me to tell her the awful truth. But then I noticed the look on her face. The pain that was there before me, displayed, was enough to show me that Mummy did not want to know that it was true. All that she was hoping for was that I would convince her that it was all untrue, that the man she had chosen to marry could not do this to his children.

Before she let me answer her stream of questions, she exclaimed, 'It *can't be true*. Daddy could never do such things to you. He just *couldn't*. In my house? Was it in my house? Tell me! I can force you to have a test you know. If you lie to me I will take you to a doctor and he will prove that you are still a virgin. I know that you lied. Tell me!'

Throughout this unending barrage of questions mingled with statements and accusations I had still not uttered a word in response. There had not been a single second in which I had been given the opportunity to speak. At the point at which Mummy stopped asking me to tell her if *it* were true or not, she then accused me of lying.

And so it went on until Grandpa interrupted her broken discourse and asked me with sorrow in his voice, 'Did your father ...' and here he hesitated, 'Did he do anything to you – ever – that he shouldn't have done?' Grandpa silenced the hysterical screaming of my mother by his one simple question.

I looked long and hard at each of them in turn before I answered his question.

'No. He didn't ... ever.' There was silence, so I added sincerely, 'I'm sorry I lied.' Shock does funny things to one. I was almost giggling at this stage – the whole situation seemed so unreal, so farcical, so unlike I had expected it to be. Not that I could categorically state what I did expect to happen. But it seemed to be the case that Mummy cared more about whether Daddy could or could not do this *to her*. The betrayal that could be potentially felt by Mummy as a result of Daddy's behaviour came out from behind the words she said to me.

I was bewildered and confused by this reaction of Mummy's. I had to deny it all for Mummy's sake. Yet even when I denied the truth behind these allegations which I had made, not one of them seemed to believe me then either. They certainly wanted to believe me, that much was clear, but they needed to be convinced that I really was a good-for-nothing liar.

'How could you be so evil as to say such things about your father?' Mummy demanded to know. 'After all that he has done for you throughout the years, after what he has given you? How could you?' Then she added as an aside, seeing that she had not hurt me enough, 'You're a spoilt brat and you know it.'

'That's why I lied – because I am a spoilt brat, I guess. I didn't realise how much trouble it would cause when I said it to the teacher. I was just angry with Daddy at the time and I wanted to get him back.'

Without allowing me to finish what I was trying to say Mummy interrupted with, 'Get him back for what? What on earth has he done to you that you felt justified in taking that sort of sick revenge on him?'

'I'm sorry, Mummy. I am really sorry for hurting you. I didn't mean to. But Daddy hurt me too. You know he does. When he beats me with his belt for misbehaviour, that really hurts but you don't care. You don't do anything. You just let him. Even when I showed you the marks on my bottom on

100

that one occasion recently, before I came in here, you said that I deserved them. You said that if I behaved better then I wouldn't have to be punished.' At this point I broke into tears.

Grandpa and Grandma also clearly had tears welling up in their eyes. But Grandpa turned to look out of the window so that he had his back to me and I was unable to see his face after this. I don't think that they had been fully aware of these beatings until that moment. I had told them that Daddy often hit me, Kara and even Anthony when we were naughty, but they had always taken me less seriously than they were taking me now.

'Is this true, Jessica?' Grandma now questioned my mother. 'Do you let him do this to her? To Lucy? After all that she has been through herself with her heart problems and everything ... you let him hit her *with a belt?*' Grandma was incredulous at this new information. The last three words were uttered in sheer disbelief.

Mummy acknowledged that it was true, that Daddy did *occasionally* punish us in this way. The emphasis was placed on the word 'occasionally'. I stood there taking this unexpected turn of events into consideration.

'Jessica, she's just a child – they all are,' interrupted Grandpa this time. 'How could you let him beat them, for God's sake? I had no idea ... When she ran away that time and came to us and said that she was being hit, I thought...' and here Grandpa's voice broke, 'that she meant the odd smack across her bottom. If I had known ... I had no idea ... that he was beating them with his belt.' Grandpa was astonished and extremely distressed at this revelation. He went on, 'I spoke to you both about it at the time. You told me that Daniel wouldn't hit the children any more. You said that he hadn't realised how traumatising it was for them to be physically punished until Lucy ran away and came to us.' Grandpa was clearly feeling guilty for sending me back home. But then, why wouldn't he have trusted my parents? It was natural that he would do so. After all, my mother is his daughter.

'Grandpa, please don't cry,' I exclaimed feeling unendurable pain at the sight of my Grandpa's tears. I felt entirely responsible for causing his anguish.

Grandpa took his handkerchief from his pocket and wiped his eyes. 'It's all right, love,' he said gently to me. 'I'm not crying, there's no need to worry about your Grandpa.' I tried to offer Grandpa a faint smile of reassurance when he said this, but the circumstances made this impossible.

There was a short silence in which no one spoke. We all seemed to be lost to our own thoughts. Mine were revolving around whether or not Mummy would ever forgive me, especially in light of this. Clearly my grandparents were not supposed to know about these frequent physical beatings, and I had inadvertently revealed it to them, and moreover forced my mother to do the same. Daddy was not going to like this one little bit.

Grandma looked towards me as though she were thinking carefully of how to phrase her next question. 'But did he *sexually* abuse you?' Grandma asked me this time.

'No, he didn't,' I claimed as convincingly as I could. I was way too afraid of my father to own up now anyway, especially as I had denied it all to the police and then to the nurses. It was going to be difficult enough to play down the physical beatings so it was imperative that they were convinced that nothing sexual had ever been done to me. Not only that, but I felt so deeply ashamed of myself that I couldn't have faced them with the disgusting facts even if I had wanted to.

Mummy asked me again if I really had made it all up, and I insisted that I had really invented the whole thing, in order to exact revenge upon Daddy. Nobody seemed to consider the fact that not much revenge can be exacted when the person who is confided in is meant to keep the information a

102

secret in the first place. This flaw in my argument seemed to be missed by all concerned, to my overwhelming relief.

'But what made you say that?' Mummy asked, still uncertain as to where the truth was to be found.

'I don't know why I said that. Really I don't. It just kind of came into my head and I knew it was a bad thing to say about someone, that's all.' That answer really would have to satisfy them because I could think of no other. Mummy and Grandma were still looking at me suspiciously, but Grandpa kept his head lowered. 'I'm sorry,' I repeated again. 'Mummy – please will you forgive me for lying?'

The tears I shed at this request were enough to convince Mummy that I really was sorry and moreover that I really had lied in the first place. 'I don't know if I can ever forgive you,' she answered immediately in the coldest, hardest tone of voice that I had ever heard her use.

They all seemed happy enough to accept my claim that I had lied about the sexual abuse on the grounds of revenge. However my grandparents, much to my surprise took a strong position regarding their belief that Daddy really ought not to be punishing me – or the other children – with his belt. They told me that in future they would make sure this didn't happen to me again.

Being their eldest grandchild and their known favourite, I probably should not have been surprised at what they said next. But I had been expecting complete rejection from my entire family, not acceptance and understanding from any of them. 'Would you like us to see if we can take you into the nearest town – Canterbury – and get some lunch? How about it, Jessica?' they addressed the last part of this question to Mummy.

'Yes sure, whatever.' Mummy had outwardly calmed down by now, and my tears had also dried.

'We won't have any further mention of this, OK?' Grandma insisted that the matter was now well and truly closed. There was great relief in knowing that this would not be mentioned again, at least for today. In my family, if something is decidedly a secret or unspoken, then an unspoken secret it will remain.

To my further surprise the nurse in charge – Will – agreed to let me go into town with my family. He asked me if that was what I wanted, and when I nodded in assent, he said that that would be fine. Grandpa suggested that we would be gone for a couple of hours at the most. It came as a shock to me that I was being given permission to leave Redfield unit – even for a couple of hours – completely without a nurse to chaperone me. However my grandparents and my mother were clearly accompanying me.

It was strange climbing into the back of Grandpa's blue estate car once again. Mummy insisted that she sat in the front passenger seat – clearly unable to tolerate my presence or to bear being physically, let alone emotionally, near to me. So Grandma sat with me in the back. I turned my attention towards the window as I so often did in car journeys and took in the scenery as Grandpa drove us through the grounds of Redfield and out through the village on our way into the city of Canterbury.

The weather was warm and it was a pleasant day to go into the town centre. Although the journey was undertaken in silence we each of us were clearly preoccupied with the content of our own minds. When Grandpa pulled into the parking area near Dane John Park, we left the car and headed towards the town centre. There was a street musician playing various old-fashioned music in the Marlowe Parade, which we could hear for a fair distance as we walked the cobbled streets of Canterbury. Grandma and Mummy walked on ahead while I stayed behind, just a few inches away from Grandpa.

Grandpa turned to me and asked if there were any shops that I would like to go in, and I chose the nearest toyshop. It was a quaint little shop that also sold cards and posters, but along the back wall was a shelf filled with numerous cuddly toys. A piglet caught my eye and I played with it while the rest of my family edged their way round this too-small shop. As we were leaving – well as Mummy and Grandma were halfway through the exit – Grandpa asked me if I would like the pig.

'Yeah, sure I would, Grandpa, I love it. Thanks,' I said, turning to him with the first genuine smile that I had smiled in quite a long while.

So Grandpa bought me the piglet and we left the store. I immediately took the soft furry pink piglet from its bag and just held it in my hand as we walked through the main street.

The grown-ups were discussing amongst themselves where we ought to go and eat, especially as we didn't have much time before I was due back at the unit anyway. We ended up in a small place known as Café Rouge where we ate pancakes and I drank Coke. Mummy had her usual Perrier while my grandparents drank their tea. The conversation was minimal in that it centred on the food and the service in Café Rouge. Little in the way of interest was directed towards me so I entertained myself with my newly acquired piglet. He learnt how to fall unnoticed from the circular mahogany table, only to be scooped up in my hands which were strategically placed beneath the table to catch him as he fell.

This little game went on for some time before Mummy, with the same pained expression on her face that I had noticed since I first looked at her that day, decided that we all ought to make a move back to the car. Grandpa paid the bill and we left.

Mummy had still not said a single word to me, and this continued until we reached the car. I was about to climb in the front to be able to sit next to Grandpa but Mummy told me that I was to sit in the back with Grandma. That was the extent of the words that passed between us on that fateful day. Even when speaking briefly to me she was unable to look at my tormented self without venomous hatred spilling over from those imploring eyes when they met mine.

Back at the unit the nurses tried to look and behave as though nothing out of the ordinary were going on in our lives. They enquired as to whether or not we had enjoyed our meal in Canterbury and I showed Will the piglet that Grandpa had bought me. Both Mummy and my grandparents were at a loss as to what to say to me so they looked at each other searchingly before Grandpa announced that they were going to be leaving now.

We hovered near the wind-battered grey door of Redfield unit and took our leave of each other there. Grandpa let me kiss him on the cheek and so did Grandma, but Mummy just walked off and sat herself inside the car while this was going on. Few words were said at parting, so I put on the bravest face that I could muster as I waved my family goodbye and wondered if I would ever see them again.

Chapter 8

I stood at the door, watching the blue Ford Mondeo estate car drive away. When the car became no more than a blue haze in the distance as Grandpa drove along the winding roads through the vast grounds of Redfield, I ventured inside the unit, alone this time.

Elaine had left earlier that morning to spend the weekend with her prospective foster parents so I decided that I would see if the older girls would let me join in with whatever they were doing. I didn't much feel like reading to myself or engaging in any solitary activity right then. I made my way over to the pool table where Siobhan and Rebecca were playing a game. It looked as though Siobhan was winning, if the dark look of annoyance mingled with frustration on Rebecca's face was anything to go by. Rebecca always was a sore loser.

'Hey, Lucy,' greeted Siobhan, flashing her white teeth at me in a big grin as she spoke.

'Hey,' I replied back, kind of at a loss as to what to say to these two older girls. They constantly hung out together while Elaine and I did the same. Nothing personal – just age differences. 'Are you winning?' I asked Siobhan mischievously.

Rebecca explained how Siobhan was only winning because she had cheated earlier on in the game. Really, according to Rebecca, Siobhan had hit the reds when she was meant to be hitting the yellows – it all became rather garbled and confused as the justifications came flowing out of Rebecca's mouth. Siobhan and I smiled at each other to humour Rebecca, and let the game continue.

I sat down on the orange chair nearest to the pool table and watched the two of them play. Siobhan did have the edge over Rebecca when you consider the fact that she is nearly six feet tall and athletically built. Siobhan is originally from the West Indies but her family immigrated to England when Siobhan was only three, so memories of her homeland are virtually non-existent.

'Hey, you cheated!' Rebecca yelled out for at least the third time since I had been sitting near the table.

'No I did not,' Siobhan declared defiantly with anger beginning to show for the first time in her voice.

Will quietly approached the pool table and asked if there were any problems with the game. 'Nah … we're just having a laugh,' claimed Rebecca.

'Well, as long as that's all it is, girls.' Having said his piece he walked back over to the dining table and resumed drinking his coffee.

Feeling bored and restless as well as overly preoccupied with the day's events – namely the intensity of the meeting with my mother, I decided to wander back out into the field. I picked up a pen and notebook that was lying on the coffee table. It was placed there for anyone to use if they wanted to make a quick note about something that came to their mind. I took it with me into the field outside and sat myself down in what I judged to be the middle of the scratchy blades of grass. Just behind Redfield there is an area almost as big as a field which is specifically allotted for the use of the staff and children in the unit. I sat myself down in the centre of this field.

The day was coming to a close now and so the sun's rays of heat were less potent. The atmosphere was becoming more chilled as opposed to the earlier mugginess of the day. I thought for a while and then I poured out my feelings into a poem. I named it 'Anguish' as that term alone best depicted my state of mind:

Anguish

Nothing – steel this pain of loss
Biting, Consuming, Eating
Devouring these remains
Fragments; splinters are retained
Disintegration – my name?
Written words while you are gone
Blood-stained tears burning inside
Tearing into this empty
Place; deserted clear space
Trying to forget you too
Obliteration; rupture
The Dark could swallow whole
If only I had all the
Right words
If only I had written
White words, retrieving, saving
Breaking, failing, fading open
Disintegration – whose name?
Adrift upon this ocean
Eternity only me
Sinks into nothingness; blue
Bloodstained tears – you came for me
You heard my cry, held that pain
Bloodstained tears – you came for me
Conditional offering
The glass shattered; the bell jar
Discarded like waste and rot
Now there is nowhere – absence
Hurts

It wasn't until 6 p.m. that I was woken up by Will and told to go inside for dinner. I must have slept on the lawn for at least two hours after writing that poem. The mental exertion drained away enough energy to put me into a deep and dreamless sleep.

When I took my place at the dining table, Rebecca and Siobhan were already seated.

'We checked on you three times,' Rebecca said loudly, to my annoyance. 'You looked just like a little baby so we didn't have the heart to wake you, and besides, the nurses said to leave you alone.' That was more likely their reason for not disturbing me, I thought to myself.

'What were you doing out there all that time anyway?' enquired Siobhan as dinner was brought over to the table. Luckily the smell of roast lamb and mint sauce distracted Siobhan and Rebecca quickly enough so that my lack of response to their questions went by unnoticed. Dinner passed by with Rebecca and Siobhan chattering animatedly about their pool games of the afternoon. The night shift were now officially on duty – Adam and Christina – so they were being given Siobhan's and Rebecca's account of the day's events. Although Will and Kate had no doubt filled them in 'officially' already.

The nurses ate with us, but I appeared to have lost my appetite and so I asked for permission to leave the table. Christina said yes to this request, 'But first put your plate on the meal trolley in the kitchen,' – which of course I would have done without being reminded. But these nurses – sometimes if they are new to their job and discover that they have a bit of power over you then they just can't help reminding you of it. It's in their nature to do so.

Quietly I slipped away from the table and left my plate on the meal trolley situated in the kitchen. Whilst in the kitchen I ripped the page from the notebook which contained my poem. I folded it neatly and held it throughout the rest of the evening. Occasionally I would glance at it again, as it expressed my feelings better than any other words that I could find that day. Then 9 p.m. came round rather quickly and we were all sent up to bed promptly by Christina. Having had the first shower, I was first to be tucked up in bed with Pooh Bear beside me. My poem was hidden discreetly on the floor of my wardrobe, beside my two pairs of shoes.

Before I knew what was happening, Adam and Christina were waking me up. They were shaking me fairly roughly to fully rouse me from my sleep. Apparently I had been screaming hysterically whilst dreaming and it had proven difficult for the both of them to wake me. On reaching consciousness I first noticed Christina's face just above me, and then I saw that Adam was standing stock still beside her. Instantly Christina told me who they were, and what they were doing to me. As she began to explain I heard Rebecca call out from her 'cell' for a nurse to come to her aid quickly. Christina offered to go to Rebecca while Adam remained behind with me.

As I looked up, beginning to awake more fully from the dream, I saw the black leather belt round his waist. In that second all I could see was the belt. My eyes rested on his belt and nothing could have convinced me that it was anyone other than Daddy standing there beside my bed. I knew that I was in trouble. The belt was threatening, warning, forbidding and forcing me. 'Please don't punish me, I'll be a good girl,' I whispered half under my breath. Fear had seized my vocal chords and I was unable even to speak properly.

He leant down, sort of crouched beside my bed, hiding his belt through this change in position. I could smell his aftershave and see his face virtually next to mine. It was not Daddy, it was Adam. I was still unsure as to what was going to happen to me though. He could only be wearing that belt because I had done something wrong. Any second now and he would be taking it off, any second now I was going to find out what I had done this time to make him angry.

111

I looked at Adam and removed my thumb from my mouth so that I could try to speak again. I sat upright but instinctively tried to back away from him further into the pillow. 'I am really sorry I have been naughty, please don't ...'

Adam interrupted me. 'Hey, kid, it's me, Adam.' He emphasised his name 'Adam' as though it made a difference which man it was standing there with a belt ready to hand in case I misbehaved. I was silenced through the fear of making him cross. Adam spoke more softly, more gently, 'Lucy, you know I always wear belts, most men do, just to keep their trousers up! It would never cross my mind to use a belt to discipline or punish you or anyone.'

After a brief pause while he let these words sink in Adam continued, 'You don't need to be afraid of me. I don't want you to be a good girl because you are afraid of me. I want you to be a good girl because you like and respect me as I do you.'

Watching his face as he spoke, hearing the sincerity in his voice combined with the unmistakable concern in his eyes gave me a glimmer of hope that maybe, just maybe, he really did mean what he was saying.

Adam remained crouching beside my bed for some time, in silence, just looking at me, waiting for a response. It started to dawn on me that he really wasn't going to do anything bad to me. 'I do ... like you and ... respect you, Adam ...' I shared.

'I know you do, kid.'

Feeling sleepy but afraid to fall asleep I asked Adam if he would read me a story. He said yes but wanted to talk to me first about my meeting earlier that day with my family. He asked if I wanted to talk about it. Which of course I didn't. But he asked anyway. 'I heard that the grandparents visited also. That was a surprise, I take it?'

'Did you know they were coming?' I enquired, suspicious that the nurses had known all along a great deal more than they revealed to me. They probably even know my future right now, but just won't tell me.

'No, Lucy, we had no idea. I assure you that you would have been the first to know had we been informed. Clearly your mother felt that she needed some moral support, yeah?' After no response Adam added, 'What would have been the point of keeping it from you in the first place? Whether you believe me or not, we are on your side, kid.'

'Yeah I guess so,' I conceded. 'Mummy hardly spoke to me, Adam. She hates me. She told me herself that she would never forgive me for what I've done.'

He reflected for a moment before he spoke. 'Maybe that's how she feels right now, but in my experience, with a bit of time, your mum may be able to accept this whole thing a bit more. Think about how shocked she must be. You will have to give her time, kid, because she doesn't know what to think right now. On the one hand you said that your father did something terrible to you and on the other hand you denied it completely. Your mother must be pretty confused, and hurting for you too.'

'No way. She is not hurting for me – she doesn't care about me at all.'

Adam gently put his hand on my arm and whispered softly, 'But she came all this way to see you didn't she?' I nodded in agreement. 'That must mean something, Lucy. Now what about that story then?'

I told Adam where to find my Pooh Bear story book on the floor of the wardrobe. Adam picked up Piglet as he noticed that he had fallen onto the floor beside my bed and he passed him to me. While Adam went to fetch a chair from the office I settled into the bedcovers with Pooh Bear and Piglet. He returned with the chair and placed it beside my bed. As he sat down he told me to try to relax and sleep now. I said goodnight and he started to read all about when Tigger first came to the forest and discovered that he doesn't like honey.

113

Adam's voice reassured me that I was not alone as I drifted off to sleep. I was not afraid of his being there right next to my bed. I was most vulnerable but I felt safe. Somehow his truth was becoming my truth too. His belt was just a belt, Adam's belt, and it would never ever be taken off to punish me.

Adam read on and on and even moved on to the next story when he saw that I was still awake. He told me to close my eyes and go to sleep properly. I wanted to please him, to show him that I could be a good girl, so I closed my eyes, put my thumb back in my mouth and fell fast asleep. I don't remember the rest of the story or even how far Adam read on to.

The following day was Sunday and Elaine was due back at some point during the day. I was anxious to discover how her weekend had gone. It wasn't too long before I found out. Just after breakfast a chap in a grey suit who looked kind of weird to me dropped Elaine off at the unit. His hair was greasy and he looked tired, or just plain worn out. There was a short conversation in the office between this chap and the head nurse, Harriet. I could see through the glass panes of the office window that Elaine's eyes were downcast and she appeared silent throughout the conversation, which was taking place around her. Elaine was wearing the same tartan skirt and white shirt that she had worn yesterday. I tried to look as though I were just reading through the usual glossy magazines as I sat at the coffee table, while I glanced repeatedly in their direction.

As the nurse led the chap out of the unit, Elaine briefly shook the hand that he extended towards her. I noticed that he did not look her in the eyes as he said his goodbyes. Elaine came and joined me at the coffee table. She said 'Hi' and sat herself down.

'How did it go with the foster parents?' I gently asked, knowing full well that this was encroaching upon her private life.

114

'Oh, you know ...' she said nonchalantly. 'Pretty much what I expected.' After a moment's hesitation Elaine revealed that she had 'had several accidents throughout the night'. Apparently this had disturbed the two younger children in turn so that the foster parents were kept awake all through the night, much to their displeasure.

Elaine disclosed this in a matter-of-fact way as though she was describing the weather forecast to me. Evidently the decision had been made to reject Elaine on the grounds of unsuitability for their family environment. The couple 'did not feel able to offer Elaine the care and attention that she required'. Her neutral reaction to this devastating decision struck me as odd in Elaine who had desperately feared that this would be the outcome but still had hoped against all logical hope that it would work out for her.

We sat together in silence for some time when suddenly Elaine spoke again. 'Lucy?' I looked directly at her in response, and she asked, 'Am I a horrible person, do you think?'

Realising where this question was coming from – namely from the endless rejections that Elaine had suffered – I instantly told her the truth as I saw it. 'No way, you are one of the nicest people that I have ever met – I mean it, Elaine. You are my first true friend.'

She shrugged her shoulders and said 'Thanks' but somehow I knew that my words had failed to register with that part of Elaine that most needed to take them on board and believe in them. There didn't seem to be much else that I could do or say to ease her obvious pain.

I was relieved when she suggested that we play pool. The head nurse agreed to hand over the cues and Elaine beat me three times out of four. Not that I let her win or anything, I don't want you thinking I'd do anything as crass as that.

Later that same evening I received a telephone call which I was expected to take in the nurses' office. Instead of vacating the office in order to give me a semblance of privacy, Adam, who was on night duty by then, just sat himself down at the desk in the far corner of the office and pretended to be engrossed in his writing. Really he was listening to my side of the conversation, I am sure of it. Otherwise the polite thing to do would have been to leave the office.

As it happened, it was my grandma on the other end of the phone. Anxious yet pleased to hear from her I tried to speak as though I couldn't have cared less whether she had phoned just then or not. It was difficult to know how to deal with this unexpected call.

However, Grandma put me out of my misery by coming to the point of her contact pretty quickly. After the usual pleasantries were exchanged such as hello and how are you, I was informed, 'Lucy, love, we have agreed to attend a family therapy session this Friday.'

Curious as to what this meant I ventured to ask, 'Who will be there? What is it for?'

Grandma took a breath before explaining to me that my parents would be attending and that the purpose was to sort out my future.

Palpitations began at the mention of my father being there – in my presence. How would I face him, now that I had let 'our' secret out? What would he say to me? Would he speak to me? These were the questions that I wanted to raise with Grandma but did not dare to broach *the* issue.

'The nurses could have told you of this agreement to meet for family therapy but we decided that it was better for you if it came from one of us.' By the phrase 'one of us' I assumed that Grandma was referring to a member of my family.

'Yeah, sure, Grandma, thanks for telling me,' I replied, not sure what my reaction ought to be. 'May I speak to Grandpa?' I asked.

Within seconds Grandpa was on the phone. 'How's it going?' he asked me in as cheery a voice as he could manage to assume.

116

'Fine, Grandpa,' I answered, doing the same.

'We will be seeing you on Friday then,' he emphasised.

'Grandpa, am I going to be put into foster care? Do Mummy and Daddy not want me any more?'

Again, silence. 'Listen we will explain everything to you on Friday, OK? Just don't worry about anything,' he added. As if that were going to be possible. The conversation ended fairly shortly afterwards as the nurse told me that I couldn't remain on the phone much longer in case someone else was trying to get through on that same line.

The rest of that week passed relatively quickly. Because I did not want the days to pass by unnoticed, they did. Before I could attend the family therapy on the Friday I had to attend personal therapy with Mr Williams on the Thursday morning at 11 a.m. During the therapy session the week before, we had discussed the police interview and how I had successfully denied my allegations. There was only fifty minutes in which to talk and the time had been predominantly taken up with reliving that traumatic experience. Mr Williams had listened intently to my account of the experience without saying much, as there was little that he could say. If only I could have been prepared for the change in the course of the therapy that day.

Mr Williams was no fool. He knew that Daddy really had hurt me, but as yet he didn't know any of the details. I had always been too afraid to share them with him in case he hated me when he found out how bad I really was. I had kind of come to like Mr Williams, especially as I saw him every week and he was always so very nice to me and everything. It would have been virtually impossible not to like him. No one had ever paid me that much individual attention before. But this time, the therapy session was somehow different. I knew that the family therapy was scheduled for the following day and terrifying thoughts of confronting Daddy were uppermost in my mind. Due to this inherent unease I paced anxiously up and down Mr Williams's office for a few minutes before I finally relaxed enough to sit myself down in my usual place – the pale pink armchair facing the door.

Mr Williams looked at me and said that he wanted me to listen very carefully to what he was about to explain. I agreed to do this. He began in a fairly official tone: 'Lucy, due to the fact that you are legally still a minor, if you choose to tell me anything that is illegal – more specifically, if you tell me about incidents which have occurred, for example with your father – then I am obliged to record this information and to pass it on to the appropriate authorities, such as the police or social services.' I looked at him aghast – I had not even decided that I was going to share any of those details with him anyway. What gave him the right to assume this, I demanded to know.

He took a long breath before continuing. 'I know that you have a lot to talk about, kiddo – there's a hell of a lot inside of you that needs to come out. This stuff *needs* to be said. I know that you are aware more than I could ever be that deep down inside of you there is a great deal of pain being locked away. Unfortunately you are constantly being forced to lock this pain up and conceal it out of fear of losing your family. I understand this, kiddo, I really do. That's why I am taking the liberty of saying this to you now.'

I could feel his eyes on me as I cast mine down towards the floor. He really knew, even though I hadn't specifically confirmed his suspicions.

'So what are you saying, Mr Williams?' I implored him to tell me, which he did willingly.

'I'm saying that if you choose to tell me about a friend of yours – any friend – who may even have had the exact same experiences as you *may* have had' – he emphasised the word 'may' so as not to be committed to knowing anything about me for certain – 'then I will be able to respect that confidentiality.'

To ascertain that I had understood him correctly, I looked

118

up at his face. His kind eyes looked saddened and concerned – for me. We understood each other in an instant. Mr Williams was offering me an opportunity to share this dreadful dark secret without the consequences of being punished for doing so.

'Are you serious?' Incredulous as it sounded, my heart told me to trust him, while my intellect was warning me to beware of trusting anyone ever again – especially with this, and even more so especially a man. I knew from my only experience of men, through my father, that they ought never to be trusted. Yet when looking into this therapist's eyes, I saw that he had no intention of hurting me. He met my gaze with compassion and *respect* for my suffering. Almost as though he knew the depth of that suffering too, maybe from some other source, but still he had suffered too at some other time in his own history. He allowed me to see that in a moment of shared empathy.

The rhythmic ticking of the clock continued unabated while I pondered his offering. It was the best he could do for me, given the circumstances. He could see that therapy was getting nowhere all the while that my freedom to speak remained blocked by society's rules.

However, on reflection how would it be possible to even discuss this issue with this man? I had no words with which to speak about the torment I had undergone at the hands of my father. Half of what he had done to me, I didn't even understand. I was too small when he started to interfere with my body to be able to have comprehended what was going on. It was only as I became older and the threats became more ominous that I started to realise that this was completely wrong and that it was somehow *sexual*. Shame, guilt and feelings of being full of dirt overcame me as I sat before Mr Williams.

The fear of Daddy's discovering that I had not kept silent about this matter yet again gripped me. Tomorrow I would have to face Daddy. We were going to be sitting together in the same room, and I felt deeply afraid that if I were to speak today then he would know it just by looking at me. I was certain of this outcome.

'Mr Williams. I only have one question for you right now … is it OK if I ask you a question?' I began hesitating before taking what might be considered a liberty. I was extremely vulnerable in relation to this powerful man, and he knew it as much as I did.

'Of course, Lucy, ask away. Don't be shy or afraid to ask me anything that's on your mind, kiddo.'

Taking him at his word, I questioned in earnest his perception of the character of a girl who could do sexual things with her own father. 'What would you think about a girl like that? Would you not agree that she is dreadfully bad and dirty?' These questions had been burning inside of me for such a long time that they almost asked themselves. I had to find an answer for sure. I trusted Mr Williams and I wanted to know if he would hate me as much as I suspected he would.

'Any child, Lucy – any child, no matter how young or old they are – any child in relation to their parents is a vulnerable and weak human being. If parents fail to protect their child then nobody else is going to do that for them. If a girl is forced into 'doing sexual things' as you put it, with her own father, then that child is completely blameless …'

Disbelieving, I interrupted, shouting; 'But how can she be blameless when she lies there in bed keeping as still as a vegetable and letting him touch her … there…? She's bad, Mr Williams, because she didn't stop him, right?'

'The child is blameless due to the very nature of being a child. A child is not meant to know the difference between right and wrong until an adult teaches them the difference. Even then, if that same adult that feeds, loves and clothes you, then puts you in a frightening situation where he is physically overpowering, then there really are not many

120

options open to that child. Keeping still and pretending it isn't happening is one way of trying to deal with the situation. Lots of children do this, Lucy. Is that what your friend did?' he added, taking me off guard so that I answered in a timid, frightened voice, remembering the times that I was completely powerless at my father's mercy.

'Yes, she was afraid that Daddy would beat her if she didn't keep still and be quiet. He said that he would punish her if she didn't do what he said.' I stopped speaking as abruptly as the words had come flowing out.

'Please … go on, kiddo, I'm here for you – not for anyone else – you're not a bad girl, Lucy, I promise you that you're not a bad girl.' He said that *I* was not a bad girl – my need to hear this temporarily overcame my fear of speaking.

'Mr Williams, I am bad.' Then, remembering our pact I corrected myself with tears falling fast down my face, 'I mean, my friend is bad because she didn't stop him – not ever.'

He leant forward in his chair to pass me a tissue while he spoke. 'Listen to me. You *couldn't* stop him, Lucy. You are a child and he is the adult. Besides this you are clearly afraid of your father. No one on this earth would think that you are to blame for what he did to you.'

Simultaneously taking in his words and understanding that although I couldn't speak of myself in this narrative, he was able to, confused me a little. I could not speak directly about 'me' – at least not without immediately retracting it – while he could address the issues that I raised with him as though they were about me because he was not the one who was making a statement, or a minor for that matter. It made therapy more interesting, I guess. Undeniably it was incredibly hard work.

'Sometimes Daddy made *her* do bad things to him too.' Quietly I let this snippet of information fall free from my lips, both relieving and restraining me instantly. I wanted to get up and run from the room, to hide my shameful self from the kind eyes of this man. Instead I remained rooted to the seat of my chair with my eyes lowered and filled with tears. I was so afraid of his reaction that I continued talking. 'I said no to Daddy many, many times ... I really said no, and tried to make him change his mind, but he hit me until I changed my mind ... so I had to do those things to him, because I was hurting real bad, Mr Williams.'

He listened to every word that I was brave enough to speak, before appealing to me to look at him rather than at the floor. I could hardly see for the tears blocking my vision anyway, but I dared not disobey him. The memories of the consequences of disobeying Daddy were too vivid in my mind right then. This disabled me from being able to disobey anyone.

'What did he hit your friend with, kiddo?' softly he asked me this question. Knowing full well to whom he was referring when he said 'your friend' I explained in between painful sobs that he hit her with his belt sometimes so that she would do bad things to him, when Mummy wasn't there. But there were times when Mummy was there and he punished her with his belt anyway – but always for misbehaviour that Mummy knew about.

That was accepted as a form of punishment at home, I explained. 'Mummy agreed to Daddy punishing us with his belt because sometimes we were really bad – I mean my friend misbehaved quite badly at times, as you know, and so my, I mean, *her* parents used to discipline her in that way. It was the only way that she could learn to be a good girl, Daddy said. He told her that he hated punishing her, but that she was always so disobedient that he was left with no alternative.'

I paused for a moment to regain my composure but managed to continue speaking after a short while. 'Mummy always agreed with Daddy on this matter, because he knew best. If Mummy got her way we would all be dreadfully spoilt, according to Daddy.'

Mr Williams appeared to be overlooking the occasional slips of the tongue when I referred directly to myself and forgot to relate these details as though they were the experiences of some imaginary friend. Although in a strange way, I did feel as though there was a part of me, which was not me, a part of me who had experienced all of this *for* me, while my real self was hiding somewhere that was still safe deep inside of me, but that would have been too weird or difficult to explain.

Chapter 9

Mr Williams listened with careful attention to each word that I uttered. Having confided in him about the severe discipline I had undergone at home, I explained that it always proved difficult to refuse Daddy for too long. The fear of his leather belt filled me with intense fear and dread of further punishment. At night-times Daddy wouldn't threaten to punish me with his belt if I showed any resistance, but he threatened something far worse.

At weekends it was not uncommon for Daddy to suggest that while Mummy took the other children into town to accompany her while she did the weekly shopping, he would remain at home with me – to look after me. Often I would hear him say how poorly or pale I looked, and that it would be better if I were kept indoors.

Of course Mummy trusted that Daddy would be looking after me while she wasn't there. However I knew that as soon as he saw the car leave the driveway and turn the corner at the end of our road, I would be living in fear for my very life. My heart condition was a good reason for me to be kept at home with Daddy on many occasions when the rest of the family were out together, either shopping or visiting grandparents.

Daddy looked so genuinely concerned about me that even I was worried that I was terribly ill on some occasions. Yet I always wondered why Daddy hurt me if I were sick, as he had claimed. It was at these times, when we were completely alone, that I would be beaten if I tried to run away from Daddy or if I tried to push his heavy body away from my smaller, defenceless frame.

Mr Williams commented, 'That must have felt as though it were a double betrayal of trust – yours as well as your mother's.'

Tears welled up in my eyes as I thought of Mummy's ignorance of this whole state of affairs, how she really didn't know anything about what was happening. 'I wanted so much to tell her, Mr Williams, but I was so scared that Daddy would kill her like he had told me many times he would do if I dared to tell anybody, especially if I told Mummy.'

'That's completely reasonable, Lucy, you were right to be afraid – I would have been too.' Mr Williams tried to appease my long-suffering mind from its guilt.

'It's not just that I was afraid of Daddy though – I was ashamed – so *ashamed* of the things that I did with *him*.'

Mr Williams explained, 'You didn't do any of these things out of choice, it was not your fault, kiddo.'

The air was hot and stuffy in the room. Almost stifling beneath the weight of the burden that I had carried with me, alone, for far too long, I resolved to disclose the core of my being to this man. Raising my eyes to meet his gaze I looked at him directly and with defiance while I confessed, 'We had sex.'

There was silence for a few seconds, but it felt as though it lasted an hour. I had thrown down the gauntlet and challenged Mr Williams. Risking everything – his kindness to me, his care, compassion and concern for this 'thing' he knew about, yet did not really know anything about at all – I had revealed the darkest secret of all to him. Clearly my trust in him had become established. After all he was such a nice man – the kind of man that I would have chosen to be my father if only I were ever given that choice.

On realising that this was going to be the entirety of my statement, Mr Williams looked at me with real tears in his eyes. His eyes met mine, as defiantly I tried to look as though I didn't care that I was so dirty and disgusting. Holding back all tears at this point, fighting off all despair, it was imperative that I didn't reveal my weakness. If he was going to reject me now then let him do it, knowing that I couldn't care less. Yet what I saw reflected back at me was anything but rejection.

Discreetly wiping away an escaped tear, Mr Williams softly, with breaking voice, offered my soul redemption. 'Thank you for being brave enough to share this with me, Lucy.' He paused as though he needed a moment to compose his own thoughts. A fly momentarily got itself caught up in the thin white nets covering the windowpane before finding its freedom again and making its escape back into the open sky. 'You were abused. That's not sex. That's not a mutual act. Even if you consented – for any reason whatsoever – it was still abuse. Your father abused you.' Letting these words bounce off me out of fear of what would happen if absorbed in all their reality, Mr Williams, noticing my dissociation from what he was saying, repeated what he had just said, adding, 'You have been abused by the one man who ought to have protected, loved and been there for you; you are innocent.'

Innocent. Innocent. Innocent. In my mind I repeated the word over and over to myself – 'Innocent'. It sounded pure and clean, original, crisp, tidy, bright, but most of all *alive*. Mr Williams was offering me back my life.

Several minutes went by in stunned silence on my part and attentive, respectful silence on the part of the therapist. Eventually the wall of my defence cracked as life flowed back into the deadliest part of my being. Where Daddy had infiltrated my being, killed off that part of me that had trusted him with the trust that only a child could have in its father, there now resurfaced a strong glimmer of hope. Here was a man, around the same age as my own father, telling me that there was nothing that I could have done in order to have prevented this from happening. Moreover, that it happened *to* me. It was all a bit much to take in and I was relieved when the ticking of the clock reminded us that we were ten minutes over time. Therapy for today was officially over ten minutes ago.

'It's time to end the session now, Lucy.' Acknowledging the therapist's words I got up to leave. I added on my way out, 'Everything I told you today was about my friend ...'

He replied, 'And everything I told you today was said to you.'

I left his room with more dignity than I had when I had arrived. My terrible dreadful deed was revealed and contrary to all that my father had told me would happen to me, I was not rejected or accused or punished. Instead I was let off from this crime against myself with someone else's heartfelt tears.

The rest of the day passed by with my mind in a state of preoccupation, hardly noticing what was going on around me at school that afternoon, or that evening back in the unit. I barely noticed Elaine's unusually cheerful self. After the evening meal was over, Elaine handed out daisy chains to everyone present, including the nurses. Apparently she had made them in the school break-time for each one of us. They were dainty and fragile offerings. Concerned not to break mine, I placed it across the palm of my hand and looked at the tiny curling white petals around the dot of yellow in the centre of the daisy. The green stems were wilting by now, but somehow their beauty was caught up in the tragedy of their transience.

At bedtime we spoke in passing about Elaine's scheduled meeting for the following Monday with her social worker.

'Judgement day is nearly here,' Elaine commented cynically.

'Judgement day is tomorrow, you mean,' I retorted without thinking.

'Oh God yeah, I'm sorry I had forgotten about your family therapy meeting ...'

There was an embarrassed silence, so I said, 'It's OK. You have your own problems to worry about, without thinking about mine too.' I couldn't quite feign the nonchalance that I had hoped to achieve by this statement as the sudden remembrance of my own day of judgement had reawoken in me fear and apprehension.

At that point Adam called out from the dorm, 'Lights out everybody.' I heard Siobhan from within her 'cell' swear in annoyance – due to the fact that she wasn't even tired – but Adam took no notice of this protest. 'Night, Elaine.' With this parting statement, Elaine went off into her own cell and closed the door behind her. By now I was already showered and dressed for bed so I switched out the dorm light and climbed into bed. Adam had returned to his office with Christina before I returned to the dorm area. In no time at all Pooh Bear and I snuggled down in bed. It was a fairly chilly night in contrast to the heat of the day, so I pulled the covers right up to my neck in an effort to keep warm.

Sleep was pulling me in and out of consciousness, but try as I might I was unable to fend off this engulfing blanket of annihilation for too long. The weakness of my body, exhausted by the hour-long, mentally draining therapy session of that morning, was demanding its rest. Finally my weak, tired body succumbed to the greater power.

In sleep the echo of his words returned to haunt me. *'If you don't stop crying I'll make it hurt more.'* Forcing back my tears in order to halt his anger, as the fire burned inside of me a few cries of pain refused to be silenced from within.

The first time there was nobody at home. Daddy had arranged the day so that Mummy and Kara would be spending it with the grandparents. Originally the plan had been for us all to go there for the day, remain for the evening meal and then return home. But that morning Daddy had decided that I looked unwell and ought to be kept in the warm. He altruistically offered to stay at home and look after me. 'They are your parents, Jessica, it's best that you go anyway. I don't mind looking after this little one.'

Mummy questioned whether Daddy really did not mind the inconvenience of spending yet another Saturday at home looking after me. 'Next week, I'll stay at home and look after Lucy if she's still poorly – it's not fair on you, that you are left to babysit all the time,' Mummy added.

Daddy reassured Mummy that he really didn't mind. 'After a week of working in that office I don't mind spending time relaxing at home with my daughter anyway,' he said sincerely. With this in mind Mummy gently kissed me goodbye and left Daddy and me alone in the house together. I was twelve years old then.

Naturally I had expected that Daddy would go through his usual routine of sending me up to my bedroom to 'lie down and rest' as he always put it. This had been the case since somewhere around the age of seven. It's impossible to remember exactly when it all started. So when he patted me gently on the bottom and said, 'Go up to your room and lie down now,' I obeyed him instantly out of fear of being punished if I refused to do so. There was always the hope that he would not walk those stairs – today at least and not enter my pink bedroom.

As I lay on my bed with my heart pounding, Daddy's footsteps pounded the staircase simultaneously. Trembling with fright, I tried to stop breathing, hoping that I would die and go away. This failed as the need for air always overcame me even before Daddy opened my bedroom door. He closed the white-painted door behind him and approached my bed. Standing beside me, he told me to get up and remove all of my clothes.

'Daddy, please no …' I began to beg.

'Do it, Lucy or I will have to punish you for your own

good.' Hesitatingly I undid the buttons of my white dress and let it slip to the floor. Daddy, in his haste for me to get undressed, virtually ripped off my underclothes and told me to lie down again on the bed. I began to cry, but did as I was told out of fear of the consequences if I refused. Being completely naked before my father increased my vulnerability.

Daddy then removed his own trousers and shorts. He looked scary standing over me with his lower half exposed in all its grotesque humanity. Averting my eyes from this horrifying sight I was gripped with fear when Daddy's hand began caressing my milky white body. He always avoided touching my scar because he knew that it was still dreadfully sore. It was and is the only part of my body that Daddy has never violated.

Frozen with terror, my fear increased when Daddy forced open my legs. Instead of just touching me this time he did something that he had never done before. He climbed directly on top of me. I thought that I was going to be crushed with his weight alone. Suddenly, without warning the most incredible pain entered my body with a violent pushing and shoving and forcing. I screamed out in agony and tried to push Daddy off from my pinned down self. My weak little arms quickly became trapped beneath his big strong hands, while I cried out in pain for him to stop. 'Daddy, Daddy, I'm going to die … you're hurting …' I screamed, the words came out jumbled and confused in my attempt to get him off me. My breathing slowed as he crushed my chest. Realising that he was pressing too hard upon me he lifted the upper half of his body slightly away from my trapped body so that I could try to breathe again.

Yet he continued to push his way through my unprotected body, to bore deeper inside me. I expected that I was going to be split open from this huge pain that I was experiencing. I really thought that I was going to die right there and then. Although I was twelve years old I had no idea what Daddy was

130

doing to me. Ironically, although I had been forced to experience sexual behaviour, it had not yet been explained to me. I had no access to any words to explain what was happening, had I even been brave enough to dare to.

Daddy was making strange noises that I had not heard him make before. They were not words but sounds, which were incomprehensible. Tears were washing my face as this pain ripped into me.

'Please … stop … please … stop … Daddy … I'm sorry…' I begged in between suffocating sobs. My body was not my own. No longer did I have a place that belonged just to me. Confused as to what was taking place inside of me, confused as to what I had done to deserve this, Daddy continued breaking me, ignoring my desperate tormented pleas for mercy.

When he was finished he pulled himself out from within me and silently gathered up his clothes. Without looking at me, Daddy left the room.

Crying on my bed, I noticed that my legs were wet so I reluctantly but gently dared to place my hand down there to see if I had wet myself. To my horror, when I brought my now wet hand up to my face to be examined, it was smeared with blood.

Hysterically I began screaming for my father. 'Daddy, Daddy, Daddy … help … I'm dying … Daddy,' I yelled as loudly as I possibly could. Frightened by this unexpected blood from a place where blood had never before appeared, I needed my father to explain its appearance to me. What had he done?

Daddy appeared again, dressed this time, as I continued to yell. Noticing the blood himself, he told me that everything was going to be OK. 'Stop crying,' he demanded of me, but this was impossible. The most that I could do was to stifle my sobbing and let my body convulse with each repressed cry.

He ran out of the room and quickly returned with tissues from the bathroom. I also heard the sound of the water running in the bathtub as he opened my bedroom door. Daddy began to wipe away the bloody mess whilst telling me to be quiet.

'It hurts … inside,' I let slip out.

'That's because you're a big girl now. This happens to all big girls, my darling. Daddy has done you a favour. If it hadn't been me then it would have been someone who didn't love you as much as I do.'

After my sobbing slowly subsided and the intensity of the pain wore off slightly, Daddy helped me up and led me by hand to the bathroom. Climbing into the bath as instructed I noticed the tinged water as the red blood polluted the cleansing liquid. Feeling faint, I attempted to wash myself while Daddy left me alone in the bathroom.

Daddy returned shortly afterwards and helped me out of the bath. He wrapped me in a huge pristine white bath towel and dried the droplets of water off of me slowly and gently. Then he led me back to my bedroom where I noticed that he had changed my soiled bed sheets for clean ones. Feeling fainter, I virtually collapsed onto the floor but Daddy caught me in time. Carrying me over to my bed he dressed me in my favourite pink pyjamas and put me to bed. The duvet was pulled up over me and Pooh Bear was placed next to me. Throughout the dreadful experience a short time earlier, Pooh Bear had been pushed onto the floor by Daddy. Now it was Daddy who was gently placing this same bear inside the bedcovers in an effort to comfort me.

To comfort myself I put my thumb in my mouth while holding tightly to Pooh Bear with my other hand. I dared to close my eyes. Daddy spoke very quietly and firmly to me, so that I opened my eyes to show that I was paying attention to this man that I was living in mortal fear of. 'You must never tell anybody about this.' He paused, then went on, speaking seriously, 'If you do tell anyone, Lucy, then I will kill you, then I will kill Mummy and then Kara.'

Anthony wasn't born then, as his expected arrival date was not set for at least another two months. I knew that Mummy had a baby inside of her because she had told us that we were going to have another little brother or sister. She was also very large by this time, and often Kara and I would be allowed to place our hands upon Mummy's tummy and feel the baby kicking – probably trying to get out.

Daddy waited for a response from me. I was still too afraid to speak, too much in shock. 'Nobody would even believe you, I can assure you. They would just think that you are a disgusting, bad little girl and nobody would be able to love you ever again – especially Mummy.' Pausing for breath, Daddy explained that he would 'deny it completely' if I so much as dared to breathe a word of this to anyone at all. It never occurred to me to doubt Daddy's threats. Anger sounded in his voice as he declared all this. Finally he asked, 'Do you understand?' so that an answer was required of me.

'Yes, Daddy, I do.' With that said, I closed my tired eyes again and drifted off into an anguished broken sleep.

I don't remember much more of the following few weeks, months or even the past year or so in as much detail as I remember that first time. Daddy continued to hurt me in this way infrequently, and usually when we were completely alone together. But when I hit the age of thirteen he started to do this to me at night-time while Mummy was asleep in their bedroom just along the hallway. If I dared to so much as cry aloud, Daddy would threaten me instantly: '*If you don't stop crying I'll make it hurt more*' – and I knew from experience that he could and he would. This was enough to make me force down the tears along with the pain that I was suffering. Looking at my curtains or the ceiling I would drift into the outside space as though I no longer occupied my own body. Psychologically it was my only available method of escape.

Calling out, 'No, Daddy … I'm sorry…' over and over alerted Adam and Christina to my recurrent nightmare. By the time they reached me I had woken myself up with my own shouting and was crying helplessly at the memory of that first time. So that was abuse. Mr Williams said that was abuse. It was always abuse. Daddy abused me. Understanding what he had done only brought with it fresh pain and anger. If I really was innocent then that meant that Daddy was guilty – that he was to blame for my suffering.

Sitting up in bed, clutching my knees to my chin in a form of self-embrace, I let the waves of anger, hatred, remorse, despair, flood my being. I barely noticed Christina leaving Adam at the foot of my bed, with his head bowed, as the rage poured out from deep within this fragile, broken body. Unashamedly I let the tears fall as, caught within this terrifying memory, the repressed feelings were freed. Angrily I chucked Pooh Bear at Adam, who let himself be hit with all the force that a distraught thirteen-year-old girl could manage.

Alternately crying, sobbing, yelling, screaming, Adam remained there with me throughout. Not once instructing me to be quiet, to stop crying, to stop protesting at the outrageous atrocities which had been done to me. Permission was silently given, by his unmoving presence. He confirmed my experience and with it the pain and self-loathing. Waves of anger would suddenly engulf my entire body so that I shrieked with all the strength left inside of me.

Eventually the incomprehensible sounds that I uttered were able to transform themselves into words. From out of my mouth I yelled to him – to my father, to Daddy – I screamed at him as though it were he sitting there at the end of my bed. 'I hate you!' Repeatedly declaring this statement screamed out all the pain I felt inside. Then these statements of distress turned into searching, pleading questions. 'You are evil. Evil. How could you? How could you do this to me? You should have killed me instead.' Throwing myself down upon the bed, aware that Adam was still there – sitting with his head still lowered at the foot of my bed – but unafraid of this silent, still, man, I looked with blurry watery vision at the dark ceiling above me. 'Daddy ... why?' the frightened child still within me called out into the dark unrevealing night. 'Why?' Piercing the cold quiet night air with a screaming burning question, which received no response, words began to fail me yet again.

Sitting up in bed once more, I crawled across the bed sheets and made my way over to Adam. He turned his head towards me and opened his arms so that I could crawl into his embrace. Burying my head in his chest, sinking into the warmth, the love, the complete acceptance that he offered me as I am, I let my tears fall onto him. Stroking my hair while I sobbed violently, with my thumb in my mouth, being held and comforted, as this body shook with the force of its pain, no words could be said to heal this hurting, wounded creature that I had become.

Slowly as the night went on, the sobs quietened down as sleep once again reclaimed me. Adam gently helped me back into bed; his warm tender hands pulled the covers up to my neck. Ensuring that Pooh Bear was tucked in beside me, he asked if I would like him to stay for a while longer. The crying had virtually subsided at this point, and except for one or two sudden shivers of pain that ran through my body inter-mittently, the emotional outburst was over. Weakly I took my thumb from my mouth to free my hand. Touching Adam's arm gently as a gesture confirming that I would like him to remain, he understood my answer to his question. Adam continued stroking my hair. I was sure that I heard him whispering, 'Good girl, there's a good girl,' as I drifted off into a more comfortable untroubled sleep.

The following morning I had to be woken by Bryony to be up and dressed in time for breakfast. Initially I expected to see Adam still beside me, as he must have remained here with me when I fell asleep. After a few moments to readjust to the fact that it was a new day now, I left my bed and headed for the shower.

Noticing that Elaine's door was still closed, I was slightly surprised as she ought to have been up by now also. Figuring that she was downstairs at breakfast already, I hurriedly took my shower and got dressed. Noticing the absence of Rebecca and Siobhan from their respective 'cells' I ran down the small flight of stairs and took my place at the unexpectedly quiet breakfast table.

Clearly there was an undeniable silence hovering over the table as I looked at Rebecca, and Siobhan looked at me. Bryony handed out our breakfasts while I pondered the possibility that the silence was caused by my disturbing behaviour throughout the night. It was then that I became aware that Elaine was absent from the table. When she had not appeared by the time Bryony and Will sat down to join us for breakfast I considered mentioning my feelings of uneasiness.

Not wanting to speak, though, I was rescued from this task when Bryony turned to address us all. 'Last night Elaine was taken ill, an ambulance was called and she was taken to hospital.' The words sank in like knives in a fresh wound.

'Last night?' Immediately the thought ran through my head that I had somehow caused her illness through my open display of emotion.

'Elaine took an overdose of tablets which she picked up at the weekend, when she was on leave,' explained Will.

'But she … is she dead?' Siobhan enquired.

'No, Christina found her while on a routine check. Elaine is recovering and will be returning to us in a day or so – just as soon as the medical hospital discharge her back into our care.' Pausing for only a moment he continued, 'When Elaine comes back to us, it is best not to mention this behaviour to her unless she brings it up first. Do you understand, girls?' We nodded as a sign that we understood.

'Elaine is feeling pretty vulnerable at the moment so we all have to look out for her and ensure that her needs are being met. Obviously we as the nurses will be doing our bit, but as her friends, the best thing that you three can do is to respect her right to keep this to herself if she chooses to do so.'

An overdose of tablets. Elaine tried to kill herself. Trying to put the two somehow disparate pieces of information together took a great deal of strength. My first real friend wanted to get away from this life, away from me, to get out of existing. Understanding the desire to kill oneself from my own experience prevented me from judging Elaine. Still, I was pleased from my own selfish standpoint that she had not succeeded – although I knew Elaine would only have attempted something like that in the first place had she been determined to see it through. So today was going to be her day of judgement too.

Due to the scheduled family therapy meeting which was to be held at 10 a.m., it was decided by the nurses that there would be little point in my attending school for just an hour. To kill the time I sat down at the coffee table and wrote a poem. Thoughts of suicide were uppermost in my mind now – maybe Elaine had the right idea after all, that there really was no point in carrying on with this life any more. What purpose could my existence serve? With this in mind I wrote:

Suicidal

Black? White?
Are choices that simple?
Nowhere between, no end, no beginning?
The thin thread between Death and Life
Who decides when it is there to be broken?

Is Death a real escape?
Or just another pathway into a worse Hell?

137

What is contained in Death?
Is it a reality? A nothingness?
Or is it life?

A lifetime of pressures,
Confined secret thoughts ...
The feeling of being trapped
By one's own mind
Is there a purpose, a reason to all this?

Questions profound and endless
Longing, begging, pleading
On bowed knee ... for an answer
Yet there is none
Frustrating the minds of the innocent
A never ending topic in life
A final explosion in death ...
An age, a soul, a life, a body. Wasted?

There must be reasons and answers
Even if for now they remain unseen
Maybe it will be too late.

Chapter 10

When I arrived at Jarvis House with the day's head nurse, Will, I was greeted at the door by the family therapist, Mrs Turner. The designated family therapy suite is situated on the ground floor at the end of the corridor where Mr Williams works, dishing out his personal therapy. Will left me at the door with Mrs Turner, informing me that he was going to be in another room – behind, of all things, a two-way mirror! Apparently there were going to be several spectators at this family farce – including my own therapist, Mr Williams.

Disgusted and annoyed, but powerless to prevent this from happening, I followed Mrs Turner into the spacious sunny room. I observed the two-way mirror to the right side of the room, over in the corner. From where I stood it was only possible to see my own reflection and that of the other things present in the room. It appeared to be a 'normal' mirror but I knew from Will's explanation that he was somewhere behind it, observing me, yet remaining unseen himself. I wondered if my family had also been made aware of our unseen observers.

Several plastic grey chairs were arranged in a circle over by the far side of the room and I noticed that my family were already seated. I managed to catch a glimpse of Mummy's lifeless light brown hair, before lowering my eyes. I took my place in the seat offered to me by Mrs Turner, attempting to fade into oblivion. I kind of believed that if I didn't look at them, then they would not be able to look at me either. If I pretended they were not there, then they wouldn't be able to know that I was there. An absurd childish logic perhaps.

We sat in silence for what felt like an eternity but was in fact probably no longer than a minute or so. The atmosphere was so tense and thick that it made me feel quite claustrophobic.

By way of introduction Mrs Turner welcomed us all to the meeting and thanked us for attending. She told us to feel free to share whatever was on our minds and to contribute anything which we felt was relevant.

Throughout her little speech I kept my gaze fixed firmly on the floor. If I stared hard enough perhaps I could somehow disappear from here and get inside the floor. At least then this awkward meeting would be over. I was too afraid to look up because I was afraid of what or who I might see there. I was apprehensive about facing them literally in case I could see rejection or hatred in their eyes.

It was not until Mrs Turner mentioned the absence of my father that I finally dared to look up at the faces of those seated around me. My grandparents were seated almost directly opposite me while my mother was seated, alone, at the left of the circle. The therapist had sat herself down directly opposite me, next to Grandpa.

Mrs Turner was a middle-aged woman, quite large and out of proportion for her small height. Her character was imposing in its very physicality, maybe due to the fact that she emphasised it with her brightly coloured patchwork dress and purple DMs, yet she did not seem to be a particularly hostile woman. However I immediately assumed that everyone present was here for the purpose of attacking my behaviour and my character. It did not occur to me that perhaps this was not going to be the case. I was not entirely wrong anyway, at least not as far as my mother was concerned.

'Your father informed us that he did not *want* to attend the meeting today,' Mrs Turner began to explain. Rudely, Mummy snapped, 'Daniel didn't see any reason why he ought to. He has to go to work – not waste his time defending himself against Lucy's lies.'

I lowered my head in shame, whilst remembering the opinion that Mummy now had of me. Mummy's disgust towards me cut deeper than any sharp object could have managed to do.

Mrs Turner allowed Mummy time in which to speak, to make herself heard. Furtively I cast a glance in Mummy's direction and saw how thin and tired she had become. Wearing her beige dress with matching open-toed shoes, her clothes hardly concealed the deterioration of her body. The suffering engraved upon Mummy's face was deep and impenetrable. It seemed as though she had not even bothered to apply her usual foundation, so that there was no colour to her pale, gaunt face. Anger at myself rose from within me. If I could have done anything to take away Mummy's pain right then, I would have done it. If Mummy had asserted that she wanted me to die, then I would not have hesitated in cutting my own throat.

Mrs Turner addressed me at this point and asked if there was anything that I wanted to say. Thinking it best to keep off the subject of my father and his refusal to attend today, I said no. Obviously I was relieved that I did not have to face him after all. Grandpa, without waiting for his turn to speak, turned to the family therapist and announced that he had something to say.

'Go ahead, please,' Mrs Turner encouraged Grandpa, who seemed to be slightly nervous, to speak.

Looking pained but with love in his eyes, Grandpa cast a brief glance in my direction. Then he looked over at Mummy, then back at me. 'Without wasting anyone's time today it's best that we get to the point,' Grandpa declared, boldly for him, I thought. He was wearing a smart light blue

141

suit and looked as though his hair had been recently trimmed. 'The point being that Lucy's mother and father have decided that they don't want her any more. Or at least as I understand the situation to be, that Jessica has refused to have Lucy back home again.' Pausing for breath while my heart sank like a lead weight on hearing this judgement, Grandpa continued to explain, 'We – her grandma and I' – Grandpa was explaining all of this to the therapist as though he were seeking her approval rather than mine – 'we have decided that we want Lucy to come and live with us – we will take care of her.'

Looking first at my Grandma then back at Grandpa to see if this was really an option, and understanding that it was, left me feeling wanted and loved by the two most faithful people in the world.

'Excellent!' I responded, excited and happy at the prospect of living with my grandparents.

Mummy looked totally unprepared for this announcement of Grandpa's, and even less prepared for my enthusiastic response to this wonderful proposal. I wasn't going to let her know that I cared about being cast out of home. It was evident that Mummy had not been consulted about this decision until now. She tried to resume her slightly unruffled composure and accept it all without affect.

'So, Jessica … what do you say to this suggestion?' gently pushed the family therapist.

'It's fine by me, I guess. Someone has to have her. If they think that they are not too old to take her on, then let them go ahead and try. She's no angel.' This, of course, was absolutely true. My behaviour could be deplorable at times. Hence my expulsion from school. 'She will just repay all your kindness with her wickedness,' Mummy added.

'Don't you care at all?' enquired Grandma, astonished at Mummy's coldness towards me and my future. 'She is your daughter after all, Jessica …'

There was no forthcoming response to this on the part of Mummy. I looked in her direction and noticed that she was sitting as still as a rod. She gave one the impression of a statue that would fall to the ground and smash into a thousand tiny pieces if she were so much as blown upon.

The tension in the air built up until it was virtually unendurable. The family therapist decided to break the now mounting silence with a question for me. 'How do you feel about this invitation to live with your grandparents?'

Ecstatically happy, of course. I loved them with all my heart. Moreover they had never done a single thing in the whole world to hurt me or to cause me any unnecessary pain. I trusted them with my life.

I relayed my feelings of gratitude and tried to hold back on the dismay that was creeping into my heart at Mummy's lack of interest or love for me. I could understand Daddy's refusal to attend today – aside from the fact that he may not want to be questioned in my presence – he was obviously very cross with me. However, Mummy, who was here physically but not emotionally, was way too difficult to understand. Why didn't she see how much I loved her? I needed her to need me, to want me to be present always, with her. I loved her so much that I could give her up to my father. I willingly consented to be torn from my mother and spend the rest of my life in exile, with my grandparents, so that Mummy's happiness would never have to be disturbed. This all seemed to be totally lost on this woman who sat there, unmoving, with nerves of steel, before me.

The rest of the session seemed rather pointless. After it was established that I was to go and live with my grandparents upon discharge from Redfield, there was not much left that could be said. However Mrs Turner did inform me that Harrington High School for Girls had confirmed their decision to take me back into the fold, so to speak. Based upon my recovery and discharge from Redfield, they would accept me back at school. Mr Steadman, the headmaster, even passed on his kindest regards. I took that with a huge pinch of salt. I had after all experienced first hand just how kind this man could be when he put his mind to it.

Grandma asked me if I would be happy living with them, as though she could really doubt that possibility! Insisting on the fact that I would be happy proved enough to convince them that there was no need to worry on that score. 'But it will be just us three – you know that don't you. Obviously Kara and Anthony won't be around quite as much as you are used to having them around.'

'But I will still see them, won't I?' Panicked by the thought that I would be forbidden any contact at all with my own siblings, I glared at Mummy and demanded an answer.

'Yes, I suppose you will have to. They will still be spending time with their grandparents. Just because you are going to be living there will not keep any of us away.'

Great, they could all come to visit and simultaneously gloat over the outcast.

It was going to be a strange set-up, with me permanently separated from my brother and sister. Especially Kara, who was now eleven. Daddy had been threatening to hurt Kara for a long time now, if I didn't comply with his wishes. I felt loyal towards my sister in so far as that I ought to be the one to protect her, and so I offered myself in an attempt to spare her. Daddy gave me the choice over whether he would hurt my sister in the exact same way that he hurt me – this would only happen if I resisted him or cried too loudly or whatever. Undoubtedly Kara had to be put first. If I could possibly save her – just save one other person from suffering this unspeakable torture – then I had to do this. My love for Kara was greater than my love for myself, and so I pleaded with Daddy not to touch her. He promised me that he wouldn't as long as I remained 'Daddy's good girl'. I wondered what would happen to her now.

144

Naturally I was preoccupied with concern for Kara when the therapist interrupted my thoughts, with the audacity to ask me if I would like to share them. If only I could have shared with them my fears for Kara and her well-being! 'I'm not thinking of anything in particular,' I lied.

With this established, Grandpa commented on the fact that he did not have all day to sit around. The therapist offered each of us a final chance to speak, but we all passed up this opportunity. Remaining seated in my chair, Mummy and my grandparents got up to leave. After shaking hands with the therapist, Grandpa and Grandma in turn leant down to kiss my cheek on their departure. Mummy did not even address me on her way out. She had to walk right past me in order to get to the exit, but still did not allow her eyes to take in my piteous state – not for a single fleeting second.

After they had vacated the room, Mr Williams and Will joined Mrs Turner and myself in the family therapy suite.

'Did you enjoy the show?' I enquired sarcastically.

'No, Lucy, it was not a show as you so eloquently phrase it. We were only observing so that we could be there but not affect the procedure by our physical presence,' explained Will, evidently patronising me.

'Whatever,' I retorted, unconvinced of the necessity of them being present at all, in any shape or disguised form. They exchanged a few brief words, congratulating the therapist on her successful job no doubt.

Mr Williams told me he would be prepared to see me later that day if I felt that I needed to talk about the morning's decision. That was a surprise, as therapy was usually tightly structured and restricted to Thursday mornings. However this unscheduled appointment wasn't going to be necessary, and I made that clear.

'I will see you next Thursday then. OK, kiddo?' he stated as he left with Mrs Turner by his side. Mr Williams had looked at me with the same kindness in his eyes that had been bestowed upon me only yesterday. I was left alone with Will.

It was agreed that I would return to Sea House School after lunch, so Will and I went back into Redfield unit where I was instructed to set the table, which task I undertook while Will disappeared into the office with Bryony – undoubtedly to discuss the morning's entertainment. It was not too long before Siobhan and Rebecca appeared, hungry and impatient for the meal to be served. It consisted of chicken burgers and chips – not exactly appetising but I was also famished by now and ate two helpings.

The conversation around the dining table centred on Elaine and how quickly she was recovering in hospital. Bryony had called the hospital earlier that morning. Apparently Elaine was merely being observed for the next twelve hours and then she would be returned home to Redfield. It was a relief to hear that she would be coming back to us soon, as I missed her very much and it had only been half a day that she had been away from us! It felt as though our unique little family had been broken up by Elaine's absence.

School dragged throughout the rest of that day, as I had to attend art class alone. Sebastian and I sat there listening to the same old Bob Dylan tapes, while I splashed paint all over coloured pieces of card. Then I had an idea.

'May I make a "Get Well" card for Elaine?'

Sebastian, who had been informed of Elaine's suicide attempt, suggested that a 'Get Well' card may not be entirely appropriate. He suggested tactfully that I made her a picture instead. After some reflection I agreed that this would be a better idea. Knowing that Elaine loved horses I sought out a picture of a horse in one of the Country and Home style magazines that Sebastian had collected in a box, for the purpose of tracing the pictures.

Sebastian handed me several sheets of tracing paper and I

helped myself to some pink card. So, pink is my favourite colour – but the point of the picture was to remind Elaine of me! Carefully and diligently I traced the outline of the great brown horse that was on the cover of the magazine that I had chosen. Its eyes were the most difficult to trace, as they just seemed to resemble black vacant holes, no matter how I tried to fill them in either with or without the relevant shading. Sebastian lent me a hand in finishing off the horse's eyes so that they didn't look quite so scary, but even Sebastian's more professional efforts proved to be relatively futile.

As the art class came to an end I gathered up my picture and said goodbye to Sebastian for the weekend. Leaving Sea House School I ran into Siobhan and Rebecca. Siobhan was wearing a bright yellow short sundress that glowed against her dark skin. Rebecca was also wearing yellow – shorts and a T-shirt – while I as usual was wearing my favourite pink dress with the bows at the side. We walked the short distance across to Redfield unit together.

Once inside the dismal unit it was decided that the closing of the day was too glorious to be wasted sitting around indoors, so we asked permission to go out into the field where I had previously written my 'Anguish' poem. Bryony and Will agreed to this request. Bryony insisted on joining us herself, as she also wanted to soak up the remainder of the day's sunshine.

After running up to the dorm and safely placing Elaine's horse picture in my wardrobe, I went outside to join the others. I sought out a private spot where I lay down and half-slept in the warmth of the sun's rays. Bryony constantly had all three of us in her view, though. Half asleep I listened to the laughter of Siobhan and Rebecca as they chased each other round the field. After a short time they asked me if I wanted to play with them – I think the game was called 'Had' but I really didn't have the energy inside me after last night's ordeal to be able to go running around a fairly large field. So

I declined their kind invitation and warned them not to trip over me as they were running dangerously close to where I was lying on the ground.

Eventually supper time arrived and with it the nurses changed over. The night shift joined us at the dining table – Adam and Christina again. Initially it was impossible for me to make eye contact or conversation with Adam after the events of the night before.

Throughout the meal Adam chatted away as he normally did, friendly as ever. He made a transparent effort to include me in the conversation when he asked if any of us had heard of an album by Bon Jovi called *These Days*. Given that I was a self-proclaimed fan of Bon Jovi it did not escape my attention that Adam was using this fact to force me into speaking to him. 'I … I have *These Days* …' My voice trailed off as I lost the courage to elaborate any further on this remarkable collection of songs. Still, I did not manage eye contact with Adam.

'What do you think of it?' he questioned me, ignoring the signs that I would rather not be drawn into a conversation.

'I think it's quite a complex album,' I offered.

Adam raised his eyebrows at me. By this time I was able to focus on his eyebrows, but still not his eyes. 'What do you mean by that?' he asked. I could almost hear the smile in his voice.

In spite of myself, I giggled, 'I don't really know! I happened to read it in a magazine somewhere and I thought it sounded really cool.'

Adam smiled when he said, 'You're full of surprises, kid!'

Siobhan shared with Adam, 'I like *Runaway*. I had never even heard of it before Lucy kept playing it, but it kind of grew on me.' I nodded in confirmation that this was the case.

'Yeah, *Runaway* was on Bon Jovi's first hit record, it is awesome.

'Ooh,' retorted Siobhan sarcastically. 'Do Bon Jovi know that we have their number one fan right here in our midst?'

'All of their fans are number one to them,' I replied quickly and curtly. Then added, 'but no, they do not even know that I exist … yet!'

'Yet!' taunted Siobhan, laughing at this childlike optimism. 'Like they would care, anyway,' she quipped. At this point Adam interrupted our exchange, probably sensing that it was about to end in tears or a loud argument.

'Why don't you clear the table please, girls?' Adam asked. Then he led by example. He stood up from his chair and carried his own plate over to the meal trolley. He turned back to face us to ensure that we were, in fact, going to follow his lead, which we did.

Siobhan, having been sufficiently distracted by this task, decided to go and watch television with Rebecca in the sitting room. Christina turned to Adam and said that she would also go and join them. As a result, I was left standing there in front of the meal trolley, alone, with Adam.

I felt awkward and looked down at the floor. 'Would you like to join me in a game of pool?' Adam enquired.

'No, thanks,' I responded automatically, not really assessing whether or not I would in fact like to play pool. 'I think I might go and watch some television as well.'

'But you detest television, Lucy…' Adam caught me out on that one. Mostly I could not stand watching television. It probably stems back from hardly ever being allowed to watch it at home. On the rare occasions that one or both of my parents consented to any of us watching a programme we were heavily supervised by them. It was not unknown for my father to switch the programme off as soon as he anticipated it was heading somewhere unsuitable for us. Ironic I know.

'Hey, come on, let's have a game,' he insisted warmly. I dared to look directly at him this time, to see his face, his

149

meaning, his intention. He looked like the same Adam to me. There was no hint of a change in him.

'All right then,' I reluctantly agreed.

We played as though there was nothing for me to be ashamed of in his presence, as though I were the very same girl in his eyes that I had always been. The very same girl in fact that he had told, 'I would be proud to have a daughter like you.' Those words still rang in my ears and sent my heart flying several planes higher each time I remembered that Adam had said this to me.

When we had finished the pool game – which, surprisingly, I won – I passed the cue back to Adam whose duty it was to lock it in the office when not in use. Looking directly into his eyes, 'Thank you,' I said.

He seemed to understand the deeper significance behind these words and he smiled back at me, 'Don't mention it.'

It was nearly 9 p.m. and we heard Christina telling the other girls that it was time for bed. So I said goodnight to Adam and made my way upstairs, ahead of Siobhan and Rebecca. I showered first and then climbed into bed with Pooh Bear and Piglet. That night I slept soundly, untroubled and without fear.

The following morning Elaine was collected from the local hospital and brought back to Redfield unit by Harriet, in the same white van that she had used to collect me from the hospital when I had suffered from my asthma attack. I was a little apprehensive about seeing Elaine again. I wasn't quite sure what to say to her. Although on one level I really did not have a problem with anyone choosing to kill themselves, I still felt deeply betrayed by Elaine's total silence on the subject prior to her taking a deliberate overdose. Just departing from someone else's life suddenly and in that self-willed way is possibly the most difficult aspect of suicide to understand. At least it must be for those who are left behind.

I mean, we were best friends, we were inseparable in this

place; yet she never so much as gave me a hint that she was going to try to end her life. I knew she was upset and disappointed and all that, but I clearly had not appreciated the extent of her inner suffering. She must feel that she has no place in the world. No home, nowhere to be. I wish that we could adopt her, but the answer would most definitely be a 'No'. It would not even be worth broaching the subject with my parents.

I went out to stand in the corridor by the doorway to wait for Harriet and Elaine to arrive back at the unit. The journey seemed to be taking them forever as the minutes just dragged by. With each passing second I grew more and more anxious.

When the white van pulled up outside, I remained where I was. Being too nervous to approach the van I just waited and watched. Harriet called out, 'Hello, dear,' to me as she got out from the driver's side and opened the noisy passenger door for Elaine. Elaine climbed down from the short step and on seeing me she ran over to where I still stood, waiting for her. She threw her arms around me and I did the same in return to her.

'I'm sorry,' she offered.

'It's OK, Elaine, there really is no need to be sorry,' I quickly reassured her. 'I understand why you did it, but I sure am glad that you are still here. I would have gone crazy without you!' We both managed a half-hearted laugh at this.

I smiled at Elaine, and on remembering the horse picture that I had made for her in that lonely art class, I ran back inside to the pool room and over to the coffee table, where I had left it for safe-keeping.

Elaine followed close on my heels to see what the rush was. As I turned around she was standing directly behind me. 'This is for you,' I explained, as I handed the picture over.

Elaine took it from me and looked at the drawing of the horse for quite some time before she spoke. 'Because you like horses,' I offered by way of explanation in case she was wondering why I had made her a picture of a horse.

'That's the nicest thing anyone has ever done for me, Lucy.'

I looked at her for a few seconds and then put my arms round her and hugged her. It was probably true. Elaine had no one in her life to care for her other than social workers and psychiatric nurses. I couldn't imagine any one of them making her a picture or hugging her when she felt sad.

Elaine went upstairs with a nurse in tow in order to take a shower, and change into some clothes. She was still wearing her night-clothes as that was all she had with her in the hospital. After about half an hour later she reappeared, looking fresher and brighter than she had when she had first arrived back at the unit. She was wearing a white dress that had been passed on from someone who had been a lot shorter than Elaine, so that her long gangly pale legs were mostly visible. Due to her recent serious suicide attempt, Elaine was now under the constant watch of a psychiatric nurse. It was Harriet who was assigned to Elaine throughout Saturday and Sunday while Will was left to keep his eye on Rebecca, Siobhan and me.

The day passed fairly uneventfully. It proved difficult to have any private conversations with Elaine as there was always a nurse within earshot and in sight of her. We were given permission to watch a film – *Desperately Seeking Susan* which starred Madonna. We all loved that film and I had already seen it four times since being admitted to Redfield. I doubt very much that my parents would have considered it suitable viewing though. There were no further discussions with Elaine about her suicide attempt or hospital stay. The other two girls tiptoed around us for a bit but, not knowing what to say to Elaine, they left us to our own devices most of the day.

It was good in a way because we had the sitting room area pretty much to ourselves; except for the nurse who was constantly with Elaine. Aside from the nurse's presence we were able to enjoy relative freedom, watch movies and listen to CDs without interruption or fear of Siobhan demanding that we play her music instead.

When the evening arrived we were advised that Elaine would not be able to call on me throughout the night, as she would have a nurse constantly in her room with her. Elaine did not like the prospect of this but I told her that I had also been forced to have a nurse in the dorm with me throughout the night after my, admittedly half-hearted, hanging attempt. It was just procedure. I think it is because she is on some kind of suicide watch. I explained to Elaine that as soon as they assess her and consider that she is no longer suicidal they will relinquish the constant supervision and allow her a bit more freedom. I was secretly hoping that all these new sanctions against her would deter her from attempting to kill herself again.

Kate was assigned to stay with Elaine throughout the remainder of the night. It was highly unlikely that a male nurse would be left to sit in a female patient's 'cell', alone, all night. As I lay in bed, drifting in and out of sleep, every so often I would hear the dull sounds of hushed voices, coming from Elaine's direction. I assumed that Elaine had suffered another accident or two and that Kate was assisting her with changing the bed.

Again I slept relatively well without any nightmares that weekend. Although my sleep was broken at times, it was due to outside noises such as those made by Kate and Elaine as they walked the corridor to collect fresh sheets and so on. The demons inside of me appeared to have subsided at least for the time being.

The following week Elaine and I spent a great deal of time in each other's company – always with a nurse present or at least near at hand, keeping a steady eye on Elaine.

She eventually confided in me that her suicide attempt was

a result of the rejection she suffered at the hands of the prospective foster parents. She knew when she stayed with them that things were not going to work out for her. This became most apparent when night-time arrived and they were short-tempered at being woken during the night by Elaine's constant bed-wetting. The terrible irony resided in the fact that the more they showed their annoyance to Elaine, the more she wet the bed out of fear of wetting the bed.

I listened to Elaine's terrible plight and sympathised with her despair. It really did seem as though she was caught up in a hopeless situation. The fact that Elaine had tried to commit suicide as a way out of it did not strike me as cowardly, but on the contrary as a brave thing to do. Through her actions Elaine had announced to the world that not having a family is worth dying for. This struck a chord deep within me too, so how could I possibly judge Elaine's actions as wrong or misguided or foolish, as indeed the nurses seemed to be doing?

On the Thursday when I attended therapy with Mr Williams we discussed Elaine's recent suicide attempt. It tended to predominate over the whole of the therapy session until he finally asked me, 'Are you thinking of committing suicide, Lucy?' Temporarily taken aback at this audacious question, I was at first unable to answer.

After reflecting for a moment or two, I answered honestly, 'No, not right now. But if I ever had to go into foster care, away from all my family, then I would definitely kill myself.'

Mr Williams accepted my candid response and asked me how I felt about going to live with my grandparents. I told him honestly that it was better than being totally abandoned by my entire family. 'At least I will still be able to see Mummy and Kara and Anthony.'

Remembering Kara, I began to feel pangs of guilt at being offered an escape route whereas she would now be trapped forever. Yet I did not feel that this needed to be spelt out to

Mr Williams, as he appeared to know already that this was my train of thought. 'Kara will understand that your parents sent *you* away, Lucy,' he reassured me. 'You're not abandoning anybody, kiddo.' So why did I feel so lousy? 'Kara is eleven, isn't she?' he enquired of me.

'Yep, just eleven!' After a pause I added, 'I love her a lot.'

'I know you do,' Mr Williams spoke reassuringly.

'I do feel that I am … you know … abandoning my own sister … that's a really terrible thing to do …'

'Really, there is no logical ground upon which you can believe that about yourself. It seems to me as though you have done your utmost to protect Kara up until now.'

'Yes, I have,' I blurted out defensively. 'But taking her away from home won't help her; it won't solve anything, and neither would making Daddy leave either. Kara loves Daddy so much that she would really never forgive me if I got him into trouble. Don't you understand? Doesn't anyone understand?'

Mr Williams sat in silence while he pondered my questions. His oatmeal coloured turtle-neck sweater set off the brown tones in his hair. His black jeans made him look slightly more youthful than the more formal style of trousers which he usually wore.

I was taken aback when Mr Williams responded with, 'Lucy, I do understand. It must be very hard to be you right now. You are caught between what is proverbially known as a rock and a hard place. Sometimes in life we have to decide whether what we sacrifice now is going to carry any meaning in the future. That's quite a difficult concept to grasp and I don't expect you necessarily to understand it.'

To be honest I didn't fully comprehend the meaning of the sacrifice stuff but I did understand that Mr Williams was not finding this situation any easier than I was. Possibly for different reasons though.

'If I did anything to instigate Daddy's removal from home

then both my brother and sister would blame me for his plight. Not to mention Mummy, who already does blame me for everything. She won't even consider for a second that I may have been telling the truth.' Mr Williams nodded his head in acknowledgement of the accuracy of my assessment.

Inside I was feeling so desperately torn. I loved my father, yet sometimes I hated him too. I hated his cruelty and his anger and the many ways in which he chose to hurt me. But through it all I needed him. I was as dependent on him for his love and approval as the rest of my family were. Without him holding us all together we would cease to function. Mummy was unable to take a train on her own or to pay a bill by herself. She was like an adult child in many ways, utterly reliant on Daddy to see her through each day safely. I could not allow myself to split our family apart. For all their sakes I had to be the one to make the sacrifice; or even to be sacrificed.

'Mr Williams, it's almost like I have to save everyone else from me, in a way.'

He waited a moment before he spoke. 'No, Lucy, that isn't the case at all. No one needs saving from you. Please believe me. You are not to feel responsible for any of this.'

Well, I sure did feel responsible for everything. I didn't bother to share this with him as I knew that he would just disagree with me. I couldn't change the way I felt inside though. No words were powerful enough to make that happen.

I returned to the subject of going to live with my grandparents. It was playing on my mind somewhat because of the possible situation that Kara may find herself in as a result of my absence. I told Mr Williams, 'Daddy said – I mean, my friend's Daddy said, that if she didn't let him do stuff to her, if she wasn't a good girl … I hesitated before continuing, 'then he would hurt Kara … I mean, her little sister.'

156

Mr Williams looked long and hard at me before he spoke. 'Lucy, that's really awful. No child should find themselves in that situation. Her Daddy knows that what he is doing is very wrong indeed. He should be sent to jail.' After a brief pause he went on, 'If there is anything that you can do to persuade your friend to tell someone she trusts about all of this then please do so, Lucy.'

Realising that I was not prepared to respond to this he lowered his voice to a softer tone and said, 'Lucy, has your friend any idea if her sister has ever been hurt in the same way by their father?'

'No! He hasn't hurt her,' I blurted out, aghast at the idea. 'Never!' At this point I picked up one of the cuddly toys that was next to me and threw it at Mr Williams. He just caught the furry bear and passed it back over to me. When I declined to take the toy from him he placed the furry white creature on the floor beside my chair. 'I'm sorry,' I offered.

'Hey, it's OK, kiddo, no harm done.' He did not seem at all angry with me for this little outburst. I was more surprised at his lack of response to my misbehaviour than I allowed him to see.

'When I go to live with my grandparents will Kara think that I abandoned her, Mr Williams?' I bravely asked of him. I was only hoping that he would have made the link between my friend's situation and my concern over my sister's predicament.

He answered, slowly, emphasising each word, 'You will not be abandoning Kara by going to live with your grandparents. As I see it you have relatively little choice. If your parents have made their decision to hand you over to your grandparents in this way then there isn't anything that you could do to persuade them to change their mind, Lucy.'

It was the sheer relief that I experienced knowing that Daddy would not be able to hurt me again, ever, that was at the root of my guilty feelings towards my sister. I was certain that he would keep his word and Kara would be the next to suffer Daddy's anger. But I could not realistically see any way to make it all go away.

After a short pause, I tentatively confided in Mr Williams, 'I do love Daddy ... you know ... I really do and that's kind of why I don't want him to go to jail or anything. Because he is my father and I love him a lot,' adding, 'and he loves me too, Mr Williams – I know that Daddy loves me because he tells me lots of times that he loves me. It's because he loves me that he hurts me.'

Mr Williams seemed to understand where I was coming from when I made this confession. 'It is perfectly normal to love your father, Lucy' – that was exactly what I needed to hear right then. Reassurance that my love for him was not the contributing factor towards his unsolicited behaviour. Therapy ended shortly after this exchange.

Walking back to school with Charlotte escorting me, I pondered in silence everything that Mr Williams and I had talked about, especially in relation to Kara. It was imperative that she didn't blame me for the rest of her life for leaving her behind with *him* like this. Yet, as far as I could see, there was no other way, no other option. As far as I was aware, Daddy had never laid a finger on Kara up to this point in time, which meant that if I got him into any sort of official trouble for his actions towards me, then Kara would indisputably be left without a loving, nurturing, all-providing father. Anthony, Kara and Mummy would obviously hold me eternally responsible. It was a Catch 22 situation to be in. If there could be any way in which I could resolve matters then the chance would not pass by unnoticed.

However, it was not going to be too long before I was given an alternative option – one where I could redeem my sister from the clutches of the devil himself and at the same time save myself from this untenable situation by returning to the place where I believed that I *ought* to be.

Chapter 11

The following evening after the therapy session, shortly before bedtime, Elaine and I were sitting beside the coffee table, chatting about the future. We were making plans to live together when we both reached the age of eighteen. Our plan was to go to London and find a place to live there. We were going to do exactly as we pleased for the rest of our lives. We considered London to be the coolest place that anyone could choose to live, and that it would be dead easy to find a job there and have a really wicked time. Elaine and I both took comfort in the certain knowledge that no matter what may happen to us in the intervening years, as soon as we hit eighteen we would be free to meet up and live together, like the sisters that we had become.

Elaine appeared to have calmed down a great deal since her recent suicide attempt. The nurses were not watching her as intently now, so that had to be a good sign in and of itself – although I don't think that she is any happier about being without a family to love and care for her. But I'm trying to show her that having real friends can be just as good, or even better. I told her once that she wouldn't like to live in my family, but somehow the way in which she looked back at me told me that she would do *anything* to live with my family. I resolved there and then not to bring this point up in conversation again.

Later on during this same Friday evening there was a

phone call for me. Kate and Will were on night duty this evening and it was Will who called me into the nurses' office. I was told that it was my mother on the line. Elaine and I exchanged worried glances before I got up from my seat in order to follow Will into the office. I walked as slowly as I could in a desperate attempt to drag out the time before I had to speak to my mother. Although I did want to speak with her, I was also concerned regarding what this unexpected telephone call could possibly be about.

Unprepared, and not having much time to react to this surprising telephone call, I warily picked up the receiver and placed it tentatively to my ear. 'Hello,' I stumbled out nervously.

'Hello,' she replied. It really was my mother's soft, gentle voice. The same intonation, the same accent – it was all there at the other end of the phone. There were a few moments of silence, as neither of us spoke after this initial acknowledgement. I was unsure as to what I was expected to say, so I said nothing. It was the fact that I had ever spoken at all that had got me into so much trouble now.

Mummy broke the silence first by enquiring, 'How are you?'

Astonished that she even cared to ask, I replied, 'Fine, thanks' – although it was all a mere pleasantry – going through the motions of some other more sociable time that we once had shared. After this was established, Mummy got straight to the point of her call.

'Daddy and I have been talking and we have reached a decision. You are not going to live with your grandparents.' That was it. Mummy announced their decision as though it were fixed in cement. I knew from past experiences that when Daddy was involved in making a decision, then the outcome was always irrevocable.

'You can't do that,' I pleaded, but to no avail.

'I think you'll find that we can, young lady, as you are our child and not theirs and therefore legally you are my responsibility – Daddy's and mine.' Mummy's voice was cold and hard as she addressed me. Determined to hurt me in every way that she could. Clearly Daddy had instructed her in what to say, though, as Mummy never usually explained reasons for their seemingly arbitrary decisions. That was mostly left to my father.

'So what is going to happen to me, then?' Anticipating that I was going to be sent into foster care against my will, I was quite taken by surprise at what Mummy said next. I had wild visions of being sent to live with some middle-aged couple who had seven other foster children, who were merely taking them in just so that they would be entitled to receive the family allowance that went with a foster child.

'Daddy and I have been speaking to the nurses recently and apparently you are making excellent progress – so they tell me,' she added slightly sarcastically. I listened with bated breath to where this was heading. 'Therefore Daddy has decided that he wants to speak to you – now, on the phone. But the nurse I just spoke to has informed me that your own father is not allowed to speak with you unless you want to speak with him.' After a pause in which I didn't realise that Mummy had been asking me for my response or consent, she demanded, 'So, do you want to speak with your father or not?'

'Of course I do,' I replied, relieved that he would deign to talk to me after all that I had put him through recently.

Within seconds his voice came down the phone line. 'Hello, Lucy,' he began.

Terrified at just the sound of his voice, I squeaked back, 'Hi, Daddy,' trembling from my head to my toes as I was confronted with his loud deep voice at the other end of the phone line. The fear that ran through my body was inexplicable, as technically I was safe, standing there in the nurses' office with Will not far from my side.

161

Daddy was much more confident when speaking to me. Without any undue hesitation, but with that air of annoyance in his voice which I instantly recognised, he began to explain my impending fate. 'Mummy and I have been discussing your recent behaviour. In light of the fact that you have been mentally ill – or emotionally disturbed – whatever you choose to call it – I can find it within myself to forget about your appalling behaviour towards me.'

I was really galled listening to this, knowing that it was all for Mummy's benefit as she would have been seated beside him in the sitting room, listening attentively to every word. I thought it best to apologise as soon as possible to try to lessen his anger, 'I am sorry, Daddy...' I began, but he would not allow me to finish my sentence. My apology, however, was genuine. I did not want to incite his anger any more than I had done already.

'We have been informed that you are well on the way to recovery now, and more importantly that your behaviour has stabilised to such an extent that you are going to be released from Redfield shortly.'

'Really?' I asked in disbelief. Released from Redfield? Nobody had discussed this possibility with me. Clearly it was left to my parents to tell me this news for a reason. It would be great to get out of here, this prison, at last. To be free once again had begun to seem as though it were an impossible dream.

Daddy refused to repeat what he had just said. It sounded to me as though he were speaking at one of his council meetings with a pre-rehearsed speech to hand. 'You are still emotionally disturbed and your behaviour is likely to fluctuate, but we have been advised that you are likely to be far more sociable and polite than you used to be. Also a little more obedient – which can only be a good thing.' Casting my mind back involuntarily to the kind of things that Daddy expected obedience in, I shivered with fear.

'To come to the point, we have agreed – that is, Mummy

and I have agreed – that it is in everyone's best interests to let you come back home to live with us. Kara and Anthony are reacting badly enough to this separation from you as it is.'

Stunned and shocked, there was a momentary horrified silence. I knew that there was no possible way out. I had sealed my fate the moment that I agreed even to talk with my father. His voice both frightened and held me enthralled by its power and charm. For all intents and purposes he was Daddy, and I loved him with the love that a child has for her Daddy.

For those past two terrible weeks I had feared that I had lost my father's love – which I needed so much. My parents were offering me back a place in their hearts and in their homes. Yet I was as much afraid as I was grateful.

'Thank you,' I spluttered, equally regretting the fact that I would not be able to live with my grandparents after all.

'Well, you don't have to thank us,' Daddy added. 'We understand that you have been really ill so we can accept that your behaviour isn't entirely your fault.'

I was curious to find out how 'ill' I had been, so I dared to ask what 'illness' I was suffering from.

'Oh, some sort of post-traumatic stress disorder,' Daddy explained, clinically. 'It's all a result of your ongoing heart problems – the heart surgery must have traumatised you a great deal more than we realised. Particularly having the pacemaker fitted. At the time when you said to us that you would rather die than have a pacemaker fitted inside you, Mummy and I just thought that you were being dramatic. We failed to understand that you were deeply traumatised by the whole idea.'

So that's how my behavioural problems were rationalised and explained away – between the nurses, Mummy and Daddy. Of course, seeing no other option other than to go along with this, I concurred that Daddy was right. 'I was quite affected by all the heart surgery – it gives me nightmares still,' I claimed.

Daddy knew exactly what my nightmares were about because he figured in them, yet he sympathised as he replied, 'Well, Mummy and I are aware of the situation – as you experienced it – now, and so we will be better able to take care of you.'

However it would be unfair and untrue to claim that the heart problems I had experienced had not 'traumatised' me in any way as Daddy had put it, as indeed the idea of having a pacemaker fitted inside of me had freaked me out somewhat at the time. I do distinctly remember begging my parents to let me die rather than forcing me to have a mechanical object placed permanently inside my body. Yet they reassured me at the time that I would thank them when I was older for making this decision over and above my wishes to die naturally.

To me, as a child of eleven, it did not seem natural to have an electrically activated heart – one that relied on a lithium battery to function. Surely my time was up and I was meant to die. I felt that interfering with nature like this could only bring about a catastrophe. I have since always felt as though I am literally living on borrowed time. My parents and Cardiologist did not share my view on this matter, hence the papers giving consent to the operation were signed by my parents. As a child of eleven I had no official or legal say over what happened to my own body.

After a short pause for breath, in which I didn't say anything, Daddy said gently, '*Kara and Anthony really miss you.*' I knew exactly what Daddy was referring to, what he was implying when he said this to me. Thoughts of Kara flooded my brain – images of Daddy devouring her like the unsuspecting innocent that she would be caused my heart to fill with pity for her. 'You do miss them, don't you?'

'Yes, very much,' I answered immediately. Finding courage from somewhere, I boldly asked, 'Daddy … will things be *different* if I come back home?' From somewhere within me I found the inner strength to ask this question. Probably the fact that thirty or so miles physically separated us at that point enabled me to be this brave.

'Yes, they will,' he asserted with conviction, and I believed him because I wanted it to be true.

Audaciously stressing my point, I asked again, 'I mean *really different?*'

Daddy, surprisingly, answered my question for the second time. 'I told you *yes*, but Mummy and I do not want this subject addressed ever again. Do you understand? It's over. You said the most dreadful things about me, and I never want to hear it mentioned again. Do you understand?' Daddy demanded to know if I were prepared to enter into our mutual pact of silence yet again. I could hear the anger rising in his voice.

'Of course, Daddy, I understand. I'm sorry I let you down,' I offered by way of an apology for betraying 'our' secret.

It was difficult to speak too openly with Daddy while the nurse, Will, was standing virtually beside me, methodically sorting through some papers in the grey tin filing cabinet as I was speaking. I was also aware of the fact that Mummy was listening to Daddy's side of the conversation too. But still, I resolved to believe my father when he promised me that things would be different at home from now on. Being a child, it's a lot more difficult to distrust your parents, especially when you love them and all.

Really, I was willing to believe Daddy because I loved him. That was the whole reason. That and the fact that I couldn't bear the thought of separation from my entire family. Kara and Anthony were still my brother and sister and I wanted to continue to grow up with them. As for my Mummy, I hoped against hope that in time she would come to a place where she could truly forgive me and maybe even forget what I had said.

The conversation on the phone could not go on for much

longer as it was nearly 9 p.m. Will pointed this out to me, by making strange signs and pointing to the big round white clock on the wall. Daddy noticed that I was not giving him my full attention and asked me what was happening. I told him that it was nearly bedtime. That said, Daddy said goodnight to me and passed the phone back to Mummy who also said a brief goodnight.

Before allowing her to hang the phone up, I quickly asked if I could speak to Kara – just to say goodnight – as she was usually sent up to bed at around 9.30 p.m. Mummy hesitated before answering me. 'Please, Mummy,' I whined. 'You know how close we are, I really miss her. Just let me say goodnight to Kara. Especially as Anthony is already in bed so I can hardly say goodnight to him.'

'It's not that simple, Lucy,' Mummy began to explain, her voice trembling as she spoke the words. 'Kara … well, Kara is in hospital herself right now. A medical hospital.'

Without allowing Mummy time to continue I demanded to know what Kara was in hospital for. 'Is she really sick, Mummy? Is she dying?'

Reassuring me that the situation was not as serious or as dire as the one that I was assuming it to be, Mummy went on to explain that Kara 'has had an accident. That's all.'

'An accident. What sort of accident? How badly hurt is she? Mummy, tell me what happened.' Raising my voice, as the concern for Kara's safety grew with each passing moment in which Mummy refused to speak, this jolted Mummy into finally answering my questions.

Uttering each word mechanically and lifelessly as though she were reading out the weather report, Mummy explained, 'Kara has broken her arm. She fell down the stairs yesterday. Due to the fact that she sustained a great deal of bruising all over her body, the doctor decided to admit her to the children's ward until she recovers. It was a very nasty fall.'

Initially I was unable to respond as the breath went from

166

my body. 'Is that all – she fell over?' I managed to get out half in a whisper, as though fighting for air.

Mummy continued as though not hearing my question, 'She's in shock and is refusing to speak at present. Her mouth is rather swollen anyway where she hit herself on landing at the bottom of the stairs. The doctor thought that to sustain such facial injuries, Kara must have hit her face against the wall as she was falling down the staircase and then landed with full impact on her face.' Mummy paused for breath and went on, 'To be honest they don't really know all the details because Kara hasn't spoken yet. The doctors have given her strong medication to kill the pain, as there is also a great deal of internal bruising. They have suggested that this could have been caused by the fall but maybe she had previously hurt herself and not told either Daddy or me about it.' Mummy waited for a moment and then said, 'Please don't worry – Kara will be home in a few weeks at the most, I should imagine. You will be home in a couple of days so we will take you to see Kara in hospital. Daddy already suggested to me earlier on today that seeing you might cheer Kara up a little as she has missed you terribly.'

After no response from me, Mummy asked, 'You do want us to take you to see Kara, don't you? We could go to the hospital straight from Redfield if you like.' Agreeing to this offer of visiting my little sister in the hospital bed where she was now lying, I quietly asked if anyone were at home when this happened.

Mummy did not seem to realise the implication of my question and answered honestly, 'Thankfully your father was at home. He was in the study when he heard her crashing down the stairs and he called an ambulance immediately. I was at the swimming club at the time. You can imagine how worried I was when I got the call that Kara had had this terrible accident.'

After a moment's reflection, Mummy added as though it

were an afterthought, 'You children are always having accidents. I remember when you were about Kara's age and you cut yourself quite badly. I noticed the blood all over your sheets in the laundry basket. I was almost hysterical when I saw them, but your father told me that he had forgotten to mention that you had cut your knee quite deeply while playing in the garden when I was out shopping. I told him off for letting you play in the garden in the first place, when you ought to have been resting on that day. The whole purpose of your staying at home was to rest as you were poorly.'

Not being able to continue this conversation with my mother any longer, I said that I had to go to bed now and I gasped out a quiet 'Goodnight' and hung the receiver up before waiting to hear a final response from Mummy.

Hanging up the receiver I almost fainted. Physically overcome by the shock of being invited back home as well as hearing the account of Kara's accident, affected my breathing. For a short while I was forced to remain seated in the nurses' office and given my Ventolin to inhale. Will would only allow me to go on up to bed when he was sure that I was not about to develop a full-blown asthma attack. It was by now nearly 9.30 – too late to discuss the recent telephone conversation with Elaine as she would have been sent to bed by now.

Will followed me up the stairs, which I hated due to the fact that he was walking behind me the whole time. When men walk behind me it always makes me feel dreadfully uncomfortable and ill at ease. This caused me to walk rather too hurriedly and exacerbated my already poor breathing condition. As soon as I was seated on my bed in the dorm Will gave me some more of my Ventolin to inhale, which I did. When my breathing returned to a semblance of normality I requested an extra pillow for the night so that I could sleep in a more upright position. This was always necessary when my asthma worsened, so Will brought another pillow to my bed.

In the meantime I took myself off to the shower, even though Kate suggested that I give it a miss just for tonight. There was no possibility of that happening. The dirt that covered me was mostly unseen by others, but I knew that it was there and so I had to do my utmost in order to remove it. Showering was the only method available to me in Redfield for cleansing my polluted, defiled body. That necessity had to be adhered to regardless of any wheezing that I was experiencing.

Prior to my admission to Redfield, cutting my wrists used to serve as a good release for the dirt that floated around inside my body. The blood itself was a powerful antidote to the pollution that infiltrated my very veins. Having undergone therapy during my time in Redfield I have come to realise that wrist-cutting is just a 'method of coping' as they call it. There are other ways in which to cope. But I have yet to find one that is as reliable as a long hot shower. The temperature of the water contributes towards how clean I am able to feel afterwards. My body needs to be a little scalded in order to peel away the residual dirt that has gathered and resurfaced upon my skin.

Having finished in the shower after at least ten minutes, with Kate standing outside calling out to me every few minutes, 'Are you all right in there?' and being satisfied with my breathless, 'Yes', I left the cubicle and vigorously towel-dried myself. Kate had brought my white pyjamas with red hearts printed all over them, over to me in the shower room, for which I was grateful as I had forgotten them in my urgency to get beneath that cleansing stream of water. Slowly pulling on my night-clothes I was again wheezing a little more seriously than I had been before I took a shower.

Kate, who had been holding my Ventolin the whole time, passed it to me quickly, demanding that I sit down on the uncomfortable wooden bench in the shower cubicle. The steam from the water irritated my lungs and I found it virtually impossible to inhale much-needed deep breaths.

After a few minutes Kate led me slowly back to the dorm. Will was waiting for us at my bedside. 'I have called a doctor out,' he informed me, 'just to check you over, kid.'

'No way!' I complained, 'You know how much I hate doctors. What did you go and do that for? They're always really mean to me.'

Will smiled patiently at this tirade, and then insisted that I get into bed and rest. Kate, with her long ginger hair falling across me, with Will's help plumped up my pillows in an effort to help me half-sit and half-lie in bed. Although the mention of a doctor had reactivated in me thoughts of Kara's current plight, I endeavoured to not think about this as I knew that there was absolutely nothing that I could do to help at this particular time. In a couple of days I would be set free from this place and then I would be able to look after my younger sister again.

We waited together for the doorbell to ring, which would announce the doctor's arrival. Will asked if there was anything that he could do for me in the meantime, so I pushed my luck and asked him if he would read a Pooh Bear story to me.

'I would, but I don't have any Pooh Bear books with me, and I don't really remember exactly how the stories go. But I could make one up,' he offered as an alternative.

'I have a Pooh Bear storybook at the bottom of my wardrobe,' I announced triumphantly. 'It's called *When We Were Six,* and is a collection of rhymes. Would you read one, please?' Will smiled and opened up the creaking wardrobe doors. He saw the book placed neatly next to my black leather buckle shoes and bent down to pick it up.

Sitting down on a chair beside my bed, he began to read to me the rhyme about a little girl called Jane. 'Have you been a good girl, Jane?' Will began reading in a funny high-pitched voice. Sitting there, he reminded me of my grandpa at a happier time of our lives. Will's cardigan was almost the same

170

as the thick brown woollen one that Grandpa wears in the winter.

The bell rang shrilly and briskly, penetrating the silence surrounding Will's quiet gentle voice as he read the verses aloud, rhyming each sentence as A.A. Milne had intended them to be rhymed. The bell pulled me back from the light sleep that I had drifted into. Kate left us both hurriedly to run downstairs and open the door for the doctor.

By this time my breathing had calmed down of its own accord, and I was pleased that the doctor would be able to see this. Kate brought in the doctor who was on call that evening – a friendly looking middle-aged woman. Wearing a smart dark-coloured suit and carrying her doctor's bag, she sat herself down beside me on my bed. Dr South was kind but firm with me, making me undo all of the buttons along my pyjama top so that she could carry out a thorough examination of my heart and lungs. After she was satisfied with what she heard at the front of my chest, she made me lean forwards so that she could listen to the back of me – apparently so that she could hear any crackles in my lungs, of which I was later informed, there were a few.

'There are too few crackles to worry about at this stage though,' Dr South explained to the nurses present. 'I think that Lucy has actually picked up a chest infection, which is subsequently playing on her asthma. In order to rectify this I am going to leave a prescription for some antibiotics.'

'I won't have to stay in bed, will I?' whining, I implored Dr South with my eyes to say no to this question.

'Well, madam, I would recommend that you get plenty of rest. Take it easy and do not tire yourself out.' Then seeing my dismay, she added, 'You don't necessarily have to stay in bed as long as you follow these guidelines.'

'Did you hear that, Will?' I demanded of the head nurse. 'I don't have to stay in bed. The doctor said, so this means that I can get up tomorrow morning!'

Smiling at me, he conceded that if I felt well enough then I could indeed get out of bed the following day. 'But now, young lady, you must rest and sleep,' Dr South affirmed sternly.

'Yes, doctor, I promise that I will,' I replied, not meaning a word of it, but determined to convince the doctor that I would obey her every command providing that I did not have to stay in bed all weekend. I could think of nothing worse than being confined to bed while everyone else would be allowed to play downstairs or out in the sunshine.

Kate and Will both left my bedside, after saying goodnight to me. 'If you need anything during the night, then just call out, OK?' Kate reminded me.

'Yes I will,' I promised. They walked with the doctor along the corridor but all that I could hear were muffled whispered words. Kate returned and passed through my dorm to get to the office, while Will led the doctor out of the building and locked up the doors behind her.

That night I managed to fall asleep intermittently. My wheezing did manage to wake me on occasions at which point I felt the need to take my inhaler. Elaine also woke me at around three in the morning but Kate and Will decided that tonight I was not going to be allowed to assist Elaine in the changing of her sheets. They had heard her footsteps approaching my dorm and came out just as she had tapped me on my arm. Kate offered, kindly, to help Elaine in my place. Elaine understood that I was feeling unwell but rejected Kate's offer to help. It was strange, I guess, but Elaine trusted only me. So she went back to her 'cell' and dealt with her accident by herself.

I lay awake thinking about Elaine for some time, when the reality of Mummy's somewhat reluctant account of Kara's accident hit me with full force. Mummy wouldn't lie to me, I told myself, in an attempt at pacifying my overactive mind. Kara probably did fall down the stairs after all; I mean, teenagers like us are clumsy all the time. Rationalisation after rationalisation went through my mind and prevented me from sleeping any more that night. At least I would be home soon and then I could keep an eye on Kara; when she is herself released from hospital, that is.

Morning arrived quickly. I was exhausted and weak when Bryony woke us all up in time for breakfast. 'Would you like to stay in bed, sweetie?' she offered me. In spite of my earlier protests I accepted this suggestion as being in my own best interest. After a few minutes Bryony returned with my antibiotics of which I swallowed a whole spoonful without complaining. For the rest of that morning I slept without waking. It was not until after lunch that I was next woken up by Bryony and again instructed to swallow a mouthful of pink liquid.

'What is it?' I asked suspiciously this time.

'It's Cefaclor,' she explained to me, 'your antibiotic as prescribed by the doctor last night.' Being allergic to Amoxil and Erythmicin meant that I was always prescribed Cefaclor for chest infections. It tasted like strawberry in a very sugary liquid so I didn't mind it all that much.

'Oh, right,' I said, instantly remembering that I was suffering with a chest infection. So that explained why I was feeling so lousy. Although I did feel that I would be able to leave my bed now that I had slept for such a long time. 'May I get up now and go downstairs?' I asked Bryony, quickly reminding her that the doctor had said just the night before that I did not have to remain in bed, so long as I rested.

'All right then, if that's what you want to do. But there'll be no rushing around or playing about, OK? You may watch television or sit and read, that's all.'

Agreeing to this, feeling within myself that I wasn't up to much else anyway, I let Bryony help me out of bed and into my white towelling Pooh Bear dressing gown. Arriving downstairs in the main room, I noticed that the others had finished their lunch and were placing their plates on the meal trolley.

'Where's mine?' I asked Bryony, who smiled and said that she had saved me a lunch and asked, redundantly I thought, if I would like to eat it now.

Taking my place at the dining table I looked around to see where Elaine was. As I did so, Bryony placed before me a bowl of hot tomato soup with some bread. For pudding there was a banana covered in custard.

'Not exactly what a sick girl would have chosen for lunch,' I commented. 'There would be at least one bar of chocolate somewhere,' I joked with Bryony. To my surprise she agreed with me.

Whilst I was finishing off my banana and custard, Elaine soon reappeared. She joined me at the dining table and asked how I felt. 'A lot better, I guess – not as tired, anyway.'

Elaine looked downcast and mournful so I endeavoured to find out why, without appearing too inquisitive, or as though I were speaking out of turn. It didn't take long for Elaine to confide in me anyway, as we had built up a strong friendship by now.

'Lucy, are you … like … leaving here soon?' It was incredible how news seemed to travel so fast round this place, even with the rules of no prying.

'How did you know about that, Elaine?' I asked.

'Well, I just kind of guessed. Remember last night when we were sitting at the coffee table and Will came over to us to tell you that your mother was on the phone. I just wondered what she could have been calling you for – especially as you told me that she had decided that she didn't want you any more – so I just put two and two together … Have I made five?' she added sorrowfully, yet hopefully.

'Well, no, you're right about my leaving here soon. That's exactly what my parents called about. Apparently they have decided that they do want me back with them after all.'

'So you can't go and live with your grandparents?' Elaine interrupted my explanation.

'No, I guess it means that I can't,' I answered, not wanting to explain all of the intricate details to Elaine. Particularly my fears about going into foster care – if, indeed, anyone would take me at the age of thirteen. Considering that Elaine knew this from her own experience, I thought it best not to remind her of the inadequacies of the social service system at this time.

Elaine tearfully looked up at me. 'Lucy, I don't want you to go, I don't want you to leave me ...' she broke off, almost in tears.

Holding her arm gently, I explained, 'Elaine, I don't want to leave you either. You will always be my friend, I promise.' I understood how she felt. Life was in a sense just perfect the way that it was right now and it seemed a shame that it all had to change, again, just when we had all managed to get used to living here in this unit, with each other.

'It's not the end of the world, though. We will still see each other. If you want to, you can come over and stay at my house. We have a guest room. In the meantime we will keep in touch by writing and we can always phone each other. Please don't be sad, Elaine – you're going to make me cry soon!' I added, trying to lighten a difficult situation.

She tried to smile and hide her pain inside, and I did the same. The rest of my dessert was left untouched, as it didn't look as appealing as it had done before this conversation. Bryony came over to the table and removed the dirty dishes on my behalf, as I was officially unwell. Noticing that Elaine and I appeared to be in the middle of something important, Bryony didn't say anything to either of us, but took the dishes away and left us alone.

Elaine's words made an impact. Not only was I going back home to live with my parents again, but also I would be leaving this place – this unit for emotionally disturbed children which now held my only friends within the same small enclosed space.

Life back outside in the real world was going to prove tough compared to the protective environment that I had become used to. Being locked in at night, although an irritation, had after all also served to lock me away from the dangers of the world beyond these walls. The prospect of returning home was simultaneously frightening and a welcome relief. Due to the fact that my parents had relented on their earlier decision to abandon me, I could not but feel joy at the unexpected turnabout on their part in welcoming me back home, now that I was officially pronounced well by the psychiatric team in charge of me. In light of Kara's accident it was imperative that I return home as quickly as possible. Daddy had promised that he wouldn't hurt me any more, and I had to believe him.

Chapter 12

It didn't take too long for the chest infection to clear. By the end of the week it had virtually disappeared. I think that maybe this was due to the fact that the nurses had ensured I took the prescribed antibiotics regularly three times a day, in spite of all protests on my part. Taking medicine was never a strong point of mine. Especially when I was on the verge of recovery, I could never see the point in continuing with a course of medicine. My parents were quite lax in supervising a course of antibiotics so I often got away with not taking my medicine.

Alongside of this, it was seen to by those in charge of me that I was getting plenty of rest. This had entailed not being allowed to attend school, but being forced to sit around all day reading, watching television or chatting to the nurses. It was during one such chat with Harriet that I was informed of the date of my release from Redfield. It was going to be on the coming Saturday. Apparently my parents had arranged with the head nurse that they would collect me sometime in the morning – probably around 10 a.m. but this would be dependent upon the traffic.

Harriet pointed out to me that there were marked differences in my behaviour now in terms of sociability with the nurses themselves as opposed to when I had first been admitted to Redfield. Initially I would barely speak to anyone, not even Elaine, although I reckon that that was largely due to the fact that I was in a completely new and strange environment, surrounded by people that I didn't know, as well as being completely estranged from my family.

The news that I was going to be returning home within a matter of days struck me as both exciting and unnerving. Uncertain as to how my parents would react to my presence when they got me home, there were moments in which I considered running away from Redfield. Thoughts of taking Elaine up on her offer to run away and live in London were tempting at such times. However, I knew deep down inside that I could not abandon my family in this manner. Aside from this, I experienced immense relief at the knowledge that it really was true – that in spite of all misbehaviour on my part and betrayals of my family, I was still going to be accepted back home.

Of course it didn't go unnoticed that neither of my parents had bothered to call me again throughout that week, but I figured that this was just going to take a bit of time. If they were willing to let me live back at home with them, then they must be willing to start talking to me again at some point. We could hardly live together in silence, could we? Besides, they were probably too busy themselves running back and forth to the hospital to visit Kara.

On rare occasions during the day I took to my bed, but always found it best to avoid sleep if at all possible. Nightmares continued unabated, but less intense than they had been when I had first been admitted to Redfield. Occasionally I would awake in a cold sweat or shivering with fear as a result of the tormenting journey that my dream had taken me on, but these happenings were becoming less and less frequent. The urges to cut my wrists were also minimal now. It appeared that the desire to hurt myself was weakened by the fact that nobody around me seemed intent on hurting me either.

Due to my improved state of health I was allowed to attend my final therapy appointment with Mr Williams on Thursday.

I was kind of apprehensive because it would be my last appointment with him while I was in Redfield. As far as I knew, arrangements had been made for me to see a therapist near where we live but it wouldn't be Mr Williams as he only works in Jarvis House.

I arrived at my therapist's office, escorted by Charlotte who usually worked the Thursday morning shift. It was another glorious hot day, with the sun beating down upon us as we strolled the short distance between Redfield and Jarvis House. I had washed my hair just that morning and was pleased that the sun was so bright as it might make my hair lighten. Not that it would ever be as golden blonde as Rebecca's beautiful hair, but hey, I could hope.

Charlotte suddenly stopped walking just before we were about to go through into the main entrance of Jarvis House. Putting her hand into her jeans pocket she pulled out a small packet. 'I've got something for you,' she announced.

'What is it?' I asked, not being able to conceal my bewilderment.

'Have a look,' Charlotte instructed. I took the packet from her and read the label on the small white box.

'Vitamin E capsules. Take one daily,' I read aloud. 'Thanks, Charlotte,' I said, smiling, 'you remembered.'

'Sure I did, sorry it took so long to get hold of them, but I didn't get much of a chance to go into town recently,' she explained. Unsure as to how true this explanation was, I was still pleased with my gift.

'Now I will have beautiful skin and nails!'

'You already do,' Charlotte retorted facetiously.

'Thanks. I mean it. Thanks.'

Charlotte and I looked at each other as she asked, 'Are you ready to go in now?'

Realising that this was going to be my last appointment with Mr Williams, I shrugged my shoulders and said honestly, 'As ready as I will ever be.'

Charlotte said, 'Good girl,' as she led me into Jarvis House and along the corridor to the now so familiar therapist's office.

When we arrived at his slightly ajar door, Charlotte left me outside. I sat down in my usual chair next to the life-giving oxygen plant. Realising that this would be the last time that I would be able to meet with Mr Williams in my entire life caused me to feel overwhelmed with sudden emotion. I was crying uncontrollably with distress when he appeared standing at the office door to invite me inside. Mr Williams was wearing his khaki trousers with matching sweatshirt. I noticed that his face looked pained as he gently held out his hand towards me as an invitation to take hold of it and allow myself to be led into his office. I declined to take his hand but resentfully got up from the chair and went into his small office of my own accord. The despair inherent in the act of parting from this man who had brought me so far on my journey through life was indescribable.

Unable to sit myself down in my usual place, the pale pink armchair remained empty on this occasion as a mark of my impending absence. Instead I sat at his feet. It seemed as though it were the only place that I could sit. It felt appropriate for me to sit down here, with my knees pulled up close beneath my chin. I wanted him to see how much he had come to mean to me. Throughout all the tears, the heartache, the screaming at him, it was imperative that he understood that my anger was never directed at him as the man that he is, but as a man *per se*.

'Lucy, how do you feel about going back home to your parents?' he gently enquired of me, having read all the reports and being fully aware of the facts without my having to explain them.

'Fine,' was my abrupt response.

'Fine?' he repeated, as though there might be more left for me to express.

'I do love my parents and Kara and Anthony – I miss them so much.' Honestly I attempted to explain my situation to him. 'I have no choice, do I? Any more than I have a choice about never seeing you again.'

Understanding and accepting the level of my despair, he remained silent for a few moments. 'Lucy, I understand why you are going back home. As I understand it, the alternative is that you will be placed in foster care via social services and thus there would be permanent separation from your family. That must be difficult for you to take on board. It's a very black and white option that they are leaving you with, kiddo.'

Reflecting for some moments, I agreed that when he put it like that, it was quite a clear-cut decision for me to make. There was no way that I was going to willingly allow myself to end up like Elaine. As for Daddy, well, he already promised me on the phone that things would be different if I went back home. That meant that I was going to be all right now. Daddy wouldn't hurt me any more, he as good as said so. I told Mr Williams this, but he looked unconvinced. Noticing this, I asked him why he didn't seem to believe me.

'I do believe you,' he reassured me. 'I have always believed you.'

Recognising the loss that was about to be forced upon me, I virtually begged Mr Williams not to leave me. 'I still need you, Mr Williams, I still need therapy. How can you leave me like this?' I implored him to answer.

'You will see another therapist, I promise, we do know that you will continue to require therapy.'

'But it won't be you,' I emphasised. He looked at me with sadness and that same look of compassion that I always saw in his eyes when he spoke.

'No, it won't be me, but I will never forget you, kiddo. We have both learnt a great deal from each other and that's what we will take away with us – that will stay with us both forever.'

'Really? You've learnt a lot from me?' I asked, surprised

that a man like him could learn anything from someone like me.

'Sure, I have.' Then he went on to say, 'You are a very special young lady and you have a long, long way to go yet in life.' It seemed as though he was indirectly telling me never to give up, not to throw the towel in, no matter what. 'You're special, kiddo, and you have many talents which I hope that you will use.' His words seemed to be floating through the air and not really registering.

The pain of this separation was proving too much to bear. 'Mr Williams, I wrote you a poem.' I passed him the now crumpled piece of white paper with smudges of black ink where my tears had fallen and blurred the writing.

'Thank you,' he said as he took this offering from me. 'Would you like me to read it now or later?'

'Now, of course,' I declared, slightly angry, 'If you read it later then I'll never know what you think of it, will I?' Without further hesitation Mr Williams began to read the poem which I had written just a few days before. I had been contemplating the end of my therapy with this man while I had been recovering from my chest infection. There wasn't much else I was allowed to do while I was ill, so I had decided that I would write down my feelings in a poem that he would be able to keep for the rest of his life – and mine. It was meant as a parting gift.

TAKING LEAVE

Desolation
Caused by the inevitable
Separation
The time for moving on has come
Unstoppable
Pushing further and further back
The years, the days

182

The minutes, hours, seconds too
Which have gone; left
Already lived now dead in deed
Dead in action
Even words retreat repressed in
Fear that mention
Will give way to memory of
These evanescent days.

Having spent some time reading and reflecting upon the poem Mr Williams gently folded the paper in half and placed it nearby on his desk. 'Thank you, Lucy, that's a very special poem and it means a lot to me that you took the time to write it and give it to me.'

'That's OK,' I answered. By now the tears were beginning to stop flowing as I saw that Mr Williams was as unlikely to forget me as I was to forget him.

'Will you do something for me, kiddo?' he asked seriously.

'Yes ... of course ... what is it?' my response was guarded as I was unsure as to where this question was leading.

'I want you to promise me that you will always remember what I have told you.'

Interrupting, 'Sure, I remember,' I reassured him.

'Seriously, Lucy ... no matter what happens when you return home, you must always remember that you are a child and your father is an adult. Nothing that he may or may not do to you is going to be your fault.'

Catching his gaze as I looked up at him from where I was seated on the soft blue carpeted floor, by his feet, I let his words reach me. 'Are you saying that even though I have agreed to go back home, you still don't think that I am a bad girl?' I asked in all sincerity.

'That's exactly what I am saying,' he responded.

'Even if ... Well, even if ... Daddy hurts me again ... it's still not my fault?' I asked in sheer disbelief that I could be

183

deemed innocent when in actual fact I was now well aware that this behaviour was wrong.

I got up from the floor and stood before him. 'Mr Williams would you ... would you ...?' Understanding my desire he stood up also and welcomed me into his arms. For what seemed like an eternity he held me. Close to his chest I could feel the rhythm of his breathing, I could hear even the quiet beating of this warm heart, as my face remained buried in his chest. The tears that were released wet his shirt but he didn't seem to mind. For a minute or two I thought that I felt his tears falling onto my hair, cleansing me with their purity, but I can't be sure. He held me tightly, in his arms. I could feel his big hands embracing me as they were placed across my back. I put my right thumb in my mouth and let him hold me with his love.

We stood like this until it was time for me to leave. The ticking of the clock reminded us both of the time. In my attempt to ignore the harsh reality of time, the silence was broken. 'Therapy is officially over,' he said softly.

'I know,' was my quiet reply as I let him release me into the vacant space that surrounded us. I couldn't hold back the tears any more than I was able to when I had first arrived.

He looked at me with tearful sad brown eyes as he told me to 'Take care'.

'You too,' I replied sincerely. 'Mr Williams – I will miss you,' I added, unsure as to whether he really knew how much I would miss him.

'I know you will. But please – give your new therapist a chance, eh?' he asked me, half-joking and half-serious as he made this request. 'You're worth the effort, Lucy.'

With that statement reverberating around inside my head, I left him, standing there, alone, free from me. 'You're worth the effort' – these words were his final offering towards mending this broken heart.

Before leaving Jarvis House I waited in the entrance way for a few minutes, attempting to compose myself before I went back to Redfield. Nobody had ever told me before that I was worth anything. It made me feel as though I really counted, that I mattered. In this great big world, there may just be a place for me too.

Stepping out into the still glorious, blinding sunshine I walked alone back to Redfield. Now that my release date was set for Saturday, the nurses were not so stringent about monitoring me constantly throughout the day. After all, there would be no reason to run away when the freedom that I desired so much was close at hand.

The smell of cut grass washed over me as I heard the lawnmower ploughing its way across the field behind the unit. The day seemed as though it were fresh and new, as I walked away from Jarvis House. I knew that I would not be returning. Without once looking back, I kept my eyes fixed firmly on Redfield as I approached its grey wooden door.

Pausing slightly as I opened the door, in an effort to ensure that I had fully regained my composure, I walked inside. Lunch was about to be served so I took my place at the dining table, and awaited the arrival of the others. Within minutes they each bundled in from school – Elaine, Siobhan and Rebecca. Rebecca was requested by Charlotte to set the table, as it was her turn to do so, which she did with the minimum of fuss. For Rebecca this was quite an achievement as she usually made a great deal of fuss about everything, particularly when she was expected to do something that might involve serving someone else.

Lunch consisted of cold chicken sandwiches in dry white bread, with crisps for dessert – it was more like a packed lunch, but nobody was about to complain. We were all hungry after our respectively busy mornings, hence we ate our lunch rather hurriedly. There was only thirty minutes before the girls had to return back to school anyway. So I was left alone again, with just the nurses for company for the next hour and thirty minutes.

Before Elaine left Redfield in order to return to school, she asked me if I was doing OK. Knowing that this morning had been my final appointment with Mr Williams was the reason for her concern. 'I'll talk to you later, yeah?' I answered.

'Of course – when I get back from school,' Elaine responded, understanding implicitly that I was not as OK as I appeared to be. Charlotte hurried the girls off to school before making herself a coffee. I was offered a drink and opted for an orange juice.

We sat down at the dining table together and drank our respective drinks. I watched the steam curling its way upward from Charlotte's coffee cup as she sipped it. Finally Charlotte spoke. 'Would you like to discuss anything, Lucy? ... Your mother left a message with us regarding your sister's accident but you haven't brought it up with anyone, so I just wondered if you'd like to talk to me,' she enquired, directly confronting me.

After some reflection I honestly replied, 'No, not right now, Charlotte.' She accepted this with what appeared to be relief, as though she felt too out of her depth to be able to cope with the situation if there had been anything I had wished to discuss with her. After all, Charlotte is only a junior nurse, so it's not too much of a surprise if she felt ill-equipped to deal with my mixed-up psyche.

'May I go upstairs and have a lie down?' I asked, feeling the need for some space and privacy of my own, and not wanting to have to lock myself in the toilets in order to get that.

'Sure, you must be worn out after this morning, hey?'

'Yes I am, I think a nap is just what I need.' Charlotte agreed to this request on the grounds that I was still recovering from my recent chest infection.

'Take it easy. If you need anything then call out. I will be popping upstairs to check on you though every now and again,' she informed me. Then, adding as an afterthought, 'Are you sure that you are all right?'

After persuading Charlotte that I really was all right, she let me leave the table and go up to my bed in the dorm for a short rest before school was over. I lay on my bed and waited patiently for Elaine to return back from Sea House School.

The day was too hot and sunny to be able to drift off to sleep, so I played around with Pooh Bear, relieving him of his little red T-shirt and then replacing it. This game began to tire me and my thoughts got the better of me. I had tried to fend them off, but it was now proving too difficult. What would I do without Mr Williams to talk to? This question raised itself of its own accord from somewhere within my unconscious. In order to fend off the anxiety that I was feeling at the loss of Mr Williams I reminded myself that I was being referred to a new therapist.

I knew, however, that this procedure itself could take up to three months, as I would just be put on the waiting list in my area. The waiting list could be as long as my entire body for all I knew. In the meantime, I would be left alone, with my parents to look after me, and to take care of all my needs.

Hopefully I would be able to behave well when I returned home and not cause either Mummy or Daddy to be angry with me at all, ever again. If only I could be the good child that they wanted me to be then everything would be all right. I was sure that Daddy would never hurt me again if he could see that I had learnt my lesson from being shut away in Redfield. It was meant to be a punishment as far as Daddy was concerned, and it had certainly been that at times.

In this manner I let my thoughts wander for the remaining time before I heard the chatter of Siobhan, Rebecca and Elaine as they arrived back at 2 p.m. from school. Well, to be specific, I heard Siobhan's loud deep laughter as Rebecca squeaked something or other which I couldn't quite catch, considering the fact that I was upstairs in the dorm while they were downstairs in the entrance way. I figured that Elaine was with them although her voice was unheard.

187

Leaving my bed I decided to join the other girls downstairs in the recreation area. Really my motive was to catch up with Elaine and have a chat with her about my departure. This goodbye thing was harder than I had expected it to be. It was really weird, because when I had first arrived at Redfield I had thought that when the day finally arrived that I could leave this place and have my freedom and life back again, it would truly be the happiest day of my life. But now it was all so near, it didn't feel that way at all. It's strange how things turn out in spite of one's plans to the contrary.

Making my way down the narrow staircase, Elaine nearly collided with me as she came running up the stairs in the opposite direction. We laughed at this unexpected meeting whilst we both attempted to speak simultaneously. We announced in unison, 'I was coming to find you!' this made us laugh some more, which caught the attention of Charlotte. She called us both downstairs to the recreation area, which we willingly obeyed.

Once downstairs we sought permission to go outside to sit in the freshly mowed field. Charlotte decided that it was not in my interest as I was still officially recovering from a chest infection. I put on my most sweet imploring face, but still Charlotte remained steadfast in her decision.

Seeing that Charlotte was not going to change her mind, Elaine and I went over and took our usual seats by the coffee table. Rebecca and Siobhan had already gone out into the field by this time, so we were left alone. Both nurses remained in their office, probably appreciating the fact that Elaine and I wanted some time to be together right now. After the usual chit-chat was exchanged that centred on meaningless enquiries referring to school and how we both were – to which the standard response of 'Fine' was the definitive verdict, we really spoke to each other as the friends that we were.

'How did the therapy go?' Elaine ventured, knowing from my earlier comment that it was a sensitive issue.

'It's gone,' I responded, trying to lighten the situation with a joke. 'It really is hard to believe that it is all over,' I began to explain. 'He – Mr Williams – meant so much to me, you know, like he was a perfect father or something, I don't think that I will ever be able to forget him.'

'But that's OK,' interrupted Elaine. 'You don't have to forget him, the time that you two spent in therapy still happened and you can always keep that – inside you,' she reasoned with me. Her argument did not seem dissimilar to that offered by Mr Williams earlier on during that day, so that I wondered if they had spoken to each other about me. But knowing that this would have been impossible, not to mention against all the rules, I did not insult Elaine by asking her if this had occurred.

'Are you going to keep in touch by writing?' she questioned.

'Nope, it's not allowed,' I answered, sorry that this was the case. 'I suppose, thinking about it logically, that if Mr Williams were to correspond with all of his patients then he wouldn't be able to find the time to do any more work.' Elaine and I smirked at the thought of Mr Williams finding himself up to his ears in stacks of letters, having to reply to each and every one.

'Elaine … we will keep in touch though, won't we? You will write to me?' I asked in earnest. 'When I told you that you are my first real friend I wasn't joking – you really are my only true friend.'

Elaine took my hand and promised that as long as she had breath in her body she would always keep in touch with me. Looking into her dark mysterious eyes, I believed her. However, I felt a certain inexplicable unease as to how long Elaine would be around on this earth – with breath in her body, as she had phrased it. Of course I did not speak these thoughts openly, but somehow Elaine seemed to know and understand my fears regardless.

'Don't ever worry about me,' she exclaimed.

'Or you me,' I responded, seriously.

'Whatever happens to me will be for the best,' Elaine went on, 'and for you too,' she offered, reassuringly. I was never quite sure just how much Elaine knew about the nature of my problems at home. Although we were best friends, it was the kind of topic that was never raised in conversation. Aside from this, the fears of rejection that festered inside of me always prevented me from telling Elaine about the kinds of things that I was forced into at home. Alongside this it was the nature of the experiences themselves, which made them ineffable.

We sat there for a considerable time, in silence, just looking at each other, and at our surroundings. Elaine as of yet, had no release date set – mainly due to the fact that she had nowhere to go to on discharge. Her short scraggy brown hair was as lifeless and wayward as ever, while her too-big red sweatshirt and jeans were serving the purpose of covering her otherwise naked body for the day.

Shortly before dinner was to be served we were asked by Kate to set the table, even though it was technically Rebecca's day for table duties. As Rebecca and Siobhan were still playing outside in the sunshine, it was a lot easier for the nurse to request that we carried out this task instead. Elaine and I placed the cutlery in its usual place and set the plates upon the table.

Throughout the meal, not much was said by either Elaine or myself. Will, who was also on night duty and had officially started his shift, chattered with Siobhan and Rebecca about the forthcoming Bon Jovi *Have a Nice Day* tour. Apparently they were going to play the first ever gig at the reopening of Wembley Stadium. Bon Jovi was the last band to perform at Wembley Stadium before it was demolished in order to be rebuilt as a state of the art Stadium. So it seems only fitting that the best band in the entire world should play at one of the best Stadium's in the whole world! The girls expressed their dismay that they would be unable to go and see them perform live, as they were still confined to Redfield for an indefinite period of time.

'But you could go, Lucy,' Rebecca suggested. 'Ask your parents if it could be a coming home present.' She laughed as she spoke, as though it were a serious possibility that my parents might just want to reward me for my release from Redfield. It struck me there and then that the transition from living here to returning home after having been institutionalised for so long, was going to make home life difficult to adjust to. I even started thinking about the faded orange curtains with the holes in them, hanging up near my bed in the dorm, and how much I would miss them.

After dinner was over and the plates were piled up on the meal trolley ready for collection by the porter, we sat down to a game of Monopoly. Will insisted that we all played this time, so I agreed to be the little homeless dog that made his way round the game board, alone and unprotected.

The game took ages to get through, as Monopoly usually does. Rebecca lost, as I had taken control of Mayfair which unfortunately for her, she kept landing on. This caused a small commotion as Rebecca's ego took yet another huge blow when this happened. So much so that I wished I had let her win, in fact. But her explosive anger was quite something. I was accused of cheating and all sorts of unpleasant comments were hurled in my direction. Will resolved the situation by sending the rest of us girls up to bed, along with Christina to chaperone us, while he took Rebecca into the office for a telling off or a talking to – whatever you choose to call it, really.

As I clambered into bed that night I fell asleep with mixed thoughts in my head. Life at Redfield was coming to an end and it was now time to move on. If Redfield had taught me anything, it had taught me to appreciate what I have. After tomorrow, I would be back at home with my family.

Chapter 13

At first I thought that Saturday was already here. I had woken up around 6 a.m. and had not realised that I still had Friday to get through before Saturday could ever arrive. Will and Kate were being silent in the office adjacent to the dorm and there were no other sounds to be heard other than the faint early morning chirping from the songbirds in the fields outside.

My thoughts drifted from one subject to another. I knew that today would be the last time that I would see Harriet, Charlotte, Adam, Christina, Rebecca, Siobhan, possibly even Elaine. For all of the heartfelt promises made between Elaine and I to keep in touch and meet up, I wasn't sure how likely it was to actually happen when we were both back outside in the real world.

Our time had been here, now. We had shared nearly four months together, within the confines of this small self-enclosed unit. I had no idea if we could even take our friendship outside of these walls. Would it be the same? Did we need Redfield both to define us as well as to facilitate our unique relationship?

I asked similar questions of my relationship with Adam. I knew that he was a nurse but still I felt drawn to him in a way that I wasn't, for instance, drawn to Will or Kate or Christina. He was naturally very fatherly towards me, even more so than Mr Williams. Adam frequently read Pooh Bear stories to help me sleep and distract me from night terrors. He also comforted me when I was most distressed and he always let me be me without fear of recrimination or punishment. I knew as I contemplated all of this that I was going to miss Adam the most.

I knew as I lay there, reflecting on what I was about to lose, that I would find it harder to leave Redfield than I could ever have imagined. But it was all too late now. I had to go. The decision was made over and above me anyway. I was never even consulted as to whether or not I wanted to leave Redfield. No one had actually asked me if I felt ready to depart from here or not. Today I would even have to pack up my small suitcase in order to be ready to leave when my parents arrive to collect me tomorrow morning. My father would not appreciate being kept waiting so it is imperative that I pack up my few belongings today. I knew that he would want to get away from here in as short a time as possible. So I had better be ready and not dawdle when he arrived.

I lay in bed for some considerable time, alone with my thoughts. I felt a sadness that was unlike any other I had experienced before. It was alien and inexplicable. It was as though I was going to the gallows and could do nothing other than resign myself to this fate and accept it complacently. Ironically, it was the only way to survive the knowledge that certain death awaited.

Thankfully I was not alone much longer as Elaine rescued me from my dark thoughts. She too had just woken up and had sneaked into the dorm to see if I were also awake at this early hour.

'Hi,' she whispered.

'Hi,' I said in reply, keeping my voice hushed so as not to alert the nurses to our clandestine meeting.

'Couldn't you sleep either?' Elaine asked quietly.

'No, I woke up about half an hour ago and couldn't get back to sleep.'

We both heard a noise from the office as though a book

had been dropped on to the floor. 'Shall we go into my room?' suggested Elaine, 'We are less likely to be overheard talking in my room. We can close the door.' I was very impressed with Elaine's practical approach to our dilemma. I am much too philosophical to be practical.

'That's an excellent idea,' I whispered back and slowly removed my bedcovers and climbed, as quietly as possible, out of bed. Elaine led the way out of the dorm, along the brightly lit corridor, to her 'cell'. Once inside she closed the door and I made myself comfortable on her bed. I had brought Pooh Bear along with me. I placed him beside me while Elaine sat herself down on her pillows with her back resting against the wall behind her bed.

'Do you want some chocolate?' she asked as she leant across to her small three drawer chest beside the bed. She opened the top drawer and pulled out a handful of chocolate bars: Milky Bar, Mars, Kit Kat and Aero. I was astonished at her collection. In all this time I had no idea that she had stored up so many sweets.

'Sure, if it's OK with you. I wouldn't say no to a Milky Bar. They are my favourite.' Elaine handed over the Milky Bar and rummaged around in the drawer for a further few seconds, producing a second Milky Bar. She gave them both to me. Then slowly Elaine picked away the shiny green foil paper from the peppermint Aero. She began to eat her way through the bubbly chocolate. We giggled because we knew that it was naughty to be eating chocolate in the early hours of the morning. The prohibition on this only added to the pleasure of doing it. It was our first midnight feast together, although it was not exactly midnight.

We didn't really talk much; we just systematically ate our way through all of the hoarded confectionery. I started to feel a bit sick halfway through but I knew that there was no going back now. We had started this together and we had to finish it together. Elaine confided in me, 'I've been saving them up for you. They are a present from me to you. I remembered that you said once that you really like chocolate but are not allowed to eat it at home.'

Feeling moved by Elaine's kindness I was even more determined that I would eat my share of the chocolates. I could not disappoint her or refuse her gift no matter how full or sick I was.

When we had munched our way through Elaine's entire chocolate collection I felt really thirsty. I asked half joking if she happened to have any water too! To my genuine surprise she leapt off the bed, opened up her wardrobe doors, and after rummaging around in the bottom of the wardrobe for a few seconds she retrieved a can of cola along with a can of traditional lemonade.

'I'm so pleased you reminded me. I had forgotten I had those hidden too,' she confided. I took the lemonade and she took the cola. It was a real treat.

'This is far better than cornflakes and toast for breakfast,' I said.

'Definitely,' Elaine agreed. We chatted about nothing in particular. Music we liked and films we wanted to see, places we would like to visit when we were older. Neither of us referred to my impending departure scheduled for the following day. It was there between us though. An almost tangible presence in the room. The more that we focused on other inane and less threatening topics the more that we hoped to make my departure from Redfield less real.

We heard the day nurses arrive. Their chatter was quite loud against the quiet upstairs. The night nurses went downstairs to hand over. Will noticed Elaine and I sitting together in her 'cell' as he passed by the corridor. He put his head in the door and said, 'Time to think about getting up now, girls.'

'Sure, we will,' Elaine replied. Then, as an afterthought, Will looked at me and said, 'See ya, Lucy, good luck, kid.'

Then he was off. Before I even had a chance to reply Will was gone. I knew that I would never see him again.

Elaine suggested that we took our showers now before Siobhan and Rebecca took over the bathroom. I went back into my dorm to collect my Pooh Bear wash bag and towel. My stomach felt heavy and bloated after all that chocolate and fizzy pop. The lethargy that had come upon me was slowing me down. I felt that my movements were less swift or agile than they could have been. If I had been allowed to I would have returned to my bed and taken a nap for a few more hours. I was really tired by now but knew that I had to get up and join the others for breakfast. I wondered if I would be allowed to attend this final day at school or not.

After enjoying the cleansing power of the hot steaming shower and changing into my white vest t-shirt and red shorts, I made my way down the stairs to the dining area. I sat alone at the table as the day nurses were talking to each other in the office and the other girls were not showered or dressed yet.

It wasn't too long before Siobhan came bounding into the room, announcing that she had decided to skip taking a shower today.

'I hope you don't smell then!' I retorted.

She playfully punched me on the top of my arm. 'I will miss you, Lucy, but if you tell anyone I said that then I will have to kill you.'

Then, before giving me time in which to respond and immediately changing the subject, she asked if I knew what we were having for breakfast. Although there is always a selection of cereals available, there are certain days that are designated as croissant and pastry days and occasionally there are even fried breakfast days. Siobhan's favourite was the fried breakfast days. I never ate fried food so on those days I stuck to my usual cereal and toast.

Shortly after, Elaine and Rebecca joined us. When Harriet

and Charlotte saw through their huge glass window that we were all seated at the dining table, waiting for our food, they decided to join us too. We were not allowed to start breakfast until everyone was seated at the breakfast table.

It was one more of the rules at Redfield. I didn't find this specific rule too difficult to remember because at home we pretty much all ate together at mealtimes as well. Except that there are certain days when Daddy has to leave the house early so that he can get to work for a meeting or something. Then he misses sitting down to breakfast with us but on those days Mummy still sits with Kara, Anthony and me. So we four always have breakfast together whether Daddy is at home or not. But at home we have muesli and certain other cereals. Mummy doesn't really approve of too much bread and certainly not fried food.

The two nurses, along with Siobhan and Rebecca, all ate their breakfast with ease. However I really struggled with just a few bites of toast. No matter how hard I tried to eat just one slice of toast I could not manage it. My stomach had still not recovered from the early morning chocolate feast with Elaine. I looked over to Elaine's plate and was amazed to see that she had eaten two slices of toast and a boiled egg. She was about to help herself to a bowl of cornflakes when Harriet asked me if I were feeling OK. 'Yes, just not very hungry, that's all.' I tried to repress a giggle when I said this.

'Hmmm, chocolate can do that to one,' Harriet winked at me when she said this. It dawned on me that the nurses had evidently realised what Elaine and I were up to but had chosen to turn a blind eye. The night nurses must have informed the day nurses at handover. I blushed red when I realised that we had been found out. But seeing no logical reason to sit at the table when I was unable to eat anything further, I asked for permission to leave the table and play some music in the sitting room. Harriet willingly consented to my request.

Whilst relaxing in the comfortable armchair and listening to Bon Jovi singing *Bad Medicine,* I could make out some slight commotion coming from the main room area. Immediately I left the sitting room with Jon Bon Jovi still singing away and went to investigate.

Harriet was physically blocking the main door whilst Charlotte was in the process of locking it. All the while this was going on there was a small slim girl of about ten or eleven standing before Harriet and screaming at the top of her lungs. She was demanding to be released this instant. With her little arms raised and her fists clenched in anger I noticed the telltale bandages around her wrists. But as I looked further up her arm there was evidence of further cuts which had healed over and formed pale scar tissue. She would be marked for life. I noticed that the child had an angelic little face with a very pale complexion and medium length blonde curly hair. Her eyes were a piercing cold blue.

Harriet just stood there calmly without responding to the girl's tantrum. She had the look of someone who had seen all this sort of behaviour before, thousands upon thousands of times, and was even expecting to see it again many more times.

When the unexpected visitor realised she was not going to be able to leave through the door, she ran over to the nearest window and tried to smash it. Lifting a chair, she was about to hurl it through the glass when Harriet grabbed the child from behind and Charlotte simultaneously wrestled the chair from her grip.

Harriet pinned the child down on to the floor and held her tightly locked, face down. The nurse didn't seem to be physically attacking the child but she was certainly firmly restraining her so that she could not move either her arms or her legs. I was shocked whilst witnessing this.

Luckily for me I had never confronted or challenged the nurses in an aggressive manner but it was evident from this display that they even had procedures for dealing with this type of behaviour, which far exceeded the punishment of being made to wear pyjamas for an indefinite length of time. If I had known that they could do this to us then I would have been far more afraid of them than I already was.

The unknown child screamed and screamed and shouted at the nurse who was still holding on to her. Harriet did not speak throughout the entire tantrum. Eventually when the child accepted that her feeble efforts to struggle free would not succeed and that she was indeed restrained, she started to cry. At first she cried just a little and asked to be let go. Harriet ignored this and continued to hold her in place.

Charlotte stepped in here and ordered Rebecca, Siobhan, Elaine and I up to the dorm. But we were all in too much shock even to move. The young girl really started to sob when it became apparent that she could not even persuade Harriet with her tears, to release her.

Charlotte spoke more sharply this time. 'Upstairs, girls,' and we instantly obeyed. The change in Charlotte's tone of voice nudged us into focusing on the potential consequences for us if we were to ignore her in favour of watching the real life drama.

Once upstairs everyone piled into the dorm area and sat on and around my bed. My bedtime story chair was still beside my bed and Siobhan sat herself down on that. I felt a little annoyed because that was my chair for the exclusive use of some of the nurses when I was fortunate enough to be read a bedtime story. Elaine sat on my bed as did I. Rebecca chose to pace up and down the room in between jumping up and down on the three other unoccupied beds.

'Whoa! Who was that?' I asked. The other girls had been in the main room area when our unexpected visitor had arrived, whereas I had been in the sitting room listening to music. I only became aware of the new arrival when she started screaming.

'She was brought in about five minutes after you left the room,' Rebecca yelled out, breathlessly, jumping high up into the air and then down again, on the bed opposite mine. 'She was protesting even then, but in more of a sulky way. Like she thought that she wasn't really going to be left here after all,' Rebecca elaborated, even more short of breath this time.

'Her parents dropped her off. Her mum is small and has blonde hair just like the girl. I didn't think much of her dad though. Really miserable looking man,' offered Siobhan. 'He hardly spoke two words to her. Just told her to behave and then walked out the door. Even though Harriet offered them tea or coffee he just said no thanks, told the girl to behave and then he walked out, with the mother following close at his heels,' Siobhan explained.

'That's awful,' I stated the obvious. 'Yeah, but we don't know what she's done to make them so angry. She doesn't look like an angel …'

'Well, actually she does,' corrected Rebecca, 'but you mean that she certainly does not behave like an angel.'

Siobhan agreed with this and added, 'And you do, I suppose?' Rebecca just carried on bouncing up and down, choosing to ignore this quip. Elaine said nothing throughout this entire discussion. But then she was always shy about talking in groups. I knew that Elaine found the two older girls quite intimidating at times. I did too occasionally, but I tried not to let them see it.

'I can't believe the way Harriet got hold of her,' I declared, still horrified at what I had just witnessed. 'I mean it was really quite vicious.' Siobhan looked in my direction and shared that she too had been held like that on several occasions when she first arrived here.

'Even your precious Adam held me like that,' she taunted. I found this difficult to comprehend. Elaine could see that I was struggling to understand what this was all about so she finally spoke up.

'It's just a common procedure that nurses here as well as social workers in the children's home are able to use when they have to deal with an aggressive child,' she explained. 'It doesn't really hurt the child, it just restrains them.'

'Usually they will do it until the child calms down and agrees to take time out.' Siobhan volunteered. 'Elaine is right, it doesn't particularly hurt, it's just really frustrating being unable to break free. That's why they do it I think, to make you calm down first.'

At this point, before I could enquire as to what 'time out' was meant to be, Harriet strolled into the dorm area with the infamous new patient standing beside her. Harriet was holding a small pink suitcase which evidently belonged to the new arrival. She turned to the blonde-haired girl and said 'Alexandra this is Siobhan, Rebecca and Elaine.'

We all said 'hi' in unison. Alexandra, however, quickly corrected Harriet with, 'Alex! My name is Alex.' I smiled at this. She was definitely a girl who knew her own mind. I admired her spirit, especially after what she had just been put through.

'OK then, Alex, which bed would you like?' Harriet indicated the three vacant beds. Rebecca had by now climbed down from her substitute trampoline and had shuffled over to be nearer to us. The new girl was making everyone feel edgy.

Alex looked around her for a few moments, taking in her surroundings, before deciding to take the bed in the far corner. The furthest away from mine. Harriet led her over there. I heard Harriet explaining to Alex the exact same thing that she had explained to me on the first day that I arrived here. Harriet was very apologetic but she would now have to search Alex's suitcase before she could have any of her things. Out of respect for Alex's privacy we were ordered by Harriet to return downstairs. We had already missed the start of school for the day as it was well after 10 a.m. by now.

When we returned to the main room Charlotte was sitting at the dining table drinking a mug of coffee. She called us over and asked us to each take a seat. 'Well, there's probably no need to tell you that we have a new admission,' she declared. 'I am assuming that you have all worked that out for yourselves.' We all nodded in agreement. 'She's called Alex and she is ten and a half. You know that's really about all that I am at liberty to tell you guys. Anything else that you may want to know, young Alex will have to tell you herself.'

We all understood the rules and were not about to protest against them. 'Seeing as you have already missed most of the school morning, Harriet and I have decided to let you have the rest of the morning off. But you will all have to go back to school after lunch. Including Alex.'

'Cool,' Siobhan announced, evidently delighted at the prospect of no school for the morning. I was not bothered either way because I never believed that I learnt anything from any of the lessons at Sea House School anyway. But I knew that Elaine would rather be in school because she really enjoyed the activities and lessons. Her experience of schools outside of here had always been brief. She had not received the best level of schooling either so Sea House School was like the equivalent of a private school for Elaine.

Rebecca asked if she could go upstairs and talk to Alex. Charlotte said that when Alex and Harriet had finished unpacking, she saw no reason why Rebecca couldn't go and properly introduce herself to Alex.

I was mystified as to why Rebecca wanted to talk to Alex first, alone. But as it happened Alex came back downstairs with Harriet and joined us at the dining table. When she was offered the chance to return upstairs alone with Rebecca, and a nurse to keep an eye on her, she declined. Alex, it appeared, was already on suicide watch and she had only just arrived. That was impressive. Although Siobhan whispered in my ear that she thought the close watch was more to do with

Alex's only being ten than with any real suicide risk. I was concerned that Alex may overhear this so I addressed her directly. 'Would you like a cup of tea? Erm, I mean orange juice perhaps?' I offered, thinking that ten year olds probably don't drink tea. I wasn't allowed even to taste tea or coffee until I was twelve. Alex opted for an orange juice and when I passed it to her she even said, 'Thank you.' This surprised me, given the outburst that I had witnessed as an introduction to this girl.

We all sat there in silence for some time until Harriet suggested that we play a game of Monopoly or Snakes & Ladders. Alex said that she preferred to play Snakes & Ladders. I went to fetch the board and we started to play. None of us really wanted to play the board game. We would rather have had some privacy and asked Alex all about herself but we knew that the nurses were not going to let that happen.

The game dragged on and we played several more until lunch time finally arrived. I don't think that anyone was really keeping score over who was winning or losing because no one really cared. Not even Rebecca.

When the lunch plates were put out before us Alex refused, point blank, to eat. We were given the choice of chicken salad sandwiches or salad sandwiches without the meat, and a packet of crisps, along with either a banana or an apple. It was quite a selection for Redfield.

Alex simply stated petulantly, 'I'm not hungry,' and refused to take a bite from anything. Neither Harriet nor Charlotte could coax her into eating. Finally Alex snapped, 'Are you going to sit on me to make me eat?'

Harriet cast a long look at Alex before answering her. 'That will depend on what you do whilst you are not eating, young lady.' After a pause Harriet went on, 'Alex, why won't you eat? Perhaps there is something else which I could try to fetch you? Would you prefer a slice of toast?'

Alex looked down at her plate. She struggled to find the

words to explain her reluctance to consume any food, but I knew that she couldn't find any way of describing what was going on inside her. Judging from how tiny she is I was beginning to think that not eating was more the norm for her than actually eating.

Alex was told to remain at the table until we had all finished eating our lunch. She didn't even try to challenge Harriet this time, but just sat there, quietly, doing as she was told.

After lunch we were all escorted across to the school building by Charlotte. As the youngest member of our unit, Alex was placed in Tim's art class with Elaine and me. We are only three years older than Alex whereas Siobhan and Rebecca are six years older. I was quite pleased for Elaine because it meant that she would not have to take her classes alone when I left. Although deep inside I was feeling a little jealous too, because Alex's arrival meant that Elaine now had someone to replace me.

The few short school hours passed relatively quickly. Alex was quite withdrawn and shy. She only spoke when spoken to, and then only briefly to answer. She was very different throughout the rest of the day, from when I first met her, mid tantrum. She was after all, only ten years old, and so it came as no surprise that she took advantage of the shiny paper and card offered by Sebastian. She made some very interesting abstract pictures for which Sebastian gave her plenty of praise. He offered to let her take them back with her to Redfield after class, 'To put on your wall?' he suggested, kindly. But Alex refused, saying that they were rubbish and she didn't want them.

The rest of the evening passed relatively uneventfully. Elaine and I spent most of the time together in the sitting room. Playing music and watching television, while Siobhan and Rebecca seemed to be taking Alex under their wing in the main room under the watchful eyes of Harriet.

At supper time we had the same ritual to observe with Alex. The night nurses were on duty now, both Adam and Christina. Neither of them could force her to eat very much. Although she did, by way of a token gesture I think, eat a small banana. The main meal of roast lamb and vegetables Alex refused so much as to look at. She definitely has issues with eating.

There were no more tantrums though. Alex sat around not talking to anyone and refusing to join in with anything. I felt sorry for her, recalling how difficult my first few days here had been. I invited her to play pool or listen to music with Elaine and me, but she refused, claiming that she did not like doing those things. Christina was constantly watching Alex, so she may have felt awkward being observed the whole time.

Elaine and I played Adam and Siobhan in a game of pool. It was the first doubles I had played since arriving here. We actually won the first two games which was a real surprise to me. Adam and Siobhan had already persuaded us to make it the best of three games and we had all agreed. So even with our first two wins behind us, we played out the final game. Elaine and I must have grown complacent due to our recent successes because they beat us easily on the third game. But Elaine and I were still the reigning champions, much to our delight.

Far too quickly 9 p.m. arrived. Christina, as usual, sent us all promptly up to bed. In that second, when I realised that I now had to go to bed, I turned to say goodnight to Adam. It was then that I realised that this would be the very last night in my entire life that I would ever say goodnight to him.

Because the day's events had kept me so busy and preoccupied, I had not even given any further thought to the fact that I was going to be leaving this place tomorrow morning. My release from here was less than twenty four hours away now. It felt odd, almost surreal. I could not imagine life outside Redfield anymore. It was like this unit was where I lived now; this place had become my home.

'Am I allowed a story tonight?' I asked Adam sweetly. 'Please ...'

He smiled at me and said, 'As it's your last night and you've been such a good girl, then yes, you are allowed a story tonight.' My face lit up at the prospect of a Pooh Bear story, read by Adam.

'Go on up to bed now, Lucy. Have the book that you want me to read ready, and I will be up shortly,' Adam said.

'OK,' I replied and virtually skipped up the stairs. After saying goodnight to Elaine, I proceeded to take the fastest and hottest shower that I could. When I had finished, barely drying myself properly, I quickly put on my pale pink nightdress. I did not want to waste a minute of extra time that I could be spending with Adam before I had to go to sleep.

When I walked into the dorm the first thing that I noticed was Alex in the bed in the far corner. She was sitting upright against the wall with her tiny legs and knees tucked under her chin. She too had a bear but it looked like a bear from a handmade bear store. I felt a little frustrated at her presence. It meant that I would not, after all, be having Adam's attention all to myself.

'Hi, Alex,' I said.

'Hi,' she said back, speaking very quietly. She sounded upset so I went over to her bed to see if there was anything that I could do for her. She had definitely been crying while I had been in the shower.

Remembering my first lonely fearful night here, I told her that I knew what she was going through. 'In my opinion,' I advised, 'you will grow to like it here too, and when you have to leave, as I do tomorrow, a part of you will actually want to stay here.'

Alex listened to me attentively, but it was clear from her expression that she was far from convinced. She did not speak to me or seem to want me to continue to talk to her so I made my way back over to my bed. I just had enough time to fetch my Pooh Bear book from the wardrobe before Adam poked his head into the dorm. 'Is it OK if I come in, girls?' he called out.

'Yes, sure it is,' I answered, speaking for both Alex and myself.

Adam walked into the dorm area, a little more cautiously, I thought, than he usually did. He looked across at Alex and asked her if she were feeling OK, to which she nodded affirmatively. 'I'm about to read a bedtime story from Lucy's Pooh Bear book now. Would you like to come over here and sit on Lucy's bed? You can hear the story with us?' Adam asked Alex, kindly.

'No thanks,' she replied. 'I don't like stories.' Adam didn't seem convinced that she didn't like stories so he suggested that she settle down inside the bedcovers and listen to the story anyway, while she fell asleep. Alex snuggled down as instructed and cuddled her bear beside her.

'Goodnight, kid,' Adam called out to her. On hearing Adam speak to Alex as he used so frequently to speak to me, made my heart jump. I knew that he would never say those words to me again.

'Shall we get on with the story now?' Adam asked, grinning at me.

I said, 'Yes!' and snuggled down inside my bed as Alex had done in hers. I placed Pooh Bear and Piglet beside me so that they could listen to the story too.

Adam opened up *The House at Pooh Corner* and began to read from the last story in the book, which was his choice. It is all about when Christopher Robin and Pooh Bear come to *An Enchanted Place* and we have to leave them there. The point of the story is that Christopher Robin and Pooh Bear have to leave each other there too. As much as he truly loves his Bear, Christopher Robin knows that he is going to be starting school soon and so he has no other choice than to say goodbye to his Bear forever. It is a very sad story and it seemed entirely appropriate that Adam chose to read this particular story on this particular night.

Halfway into the story I sat up in bed and interrupted Adam. 'I am going to miss you,' I announced, suddenly. I lowered my eyes after declaring this in case he was going to tell me how silly I was being.

He stopped reading the story and laid the book down on the corner of my bed. 'I know, Lucy. I will miss you too. But this is a new chapter in your life now, a new beginning. You have the rest of your life ahead of you. As you get older and go on through school and university you will be able to make your life your own. You will go far, kid. I have every faith in you.'

I had not been prepared for such kind and supportive words. Up until then I had not truly appreciated what I had come to mean to Adam. I had only seen our unequal relationship from my perspective and, in turn, experienced how much he meant to me. Clearly it was mutual, I evidently meant a great deal to him also. All of the respect trust and even love that we had nurtured between us was real on both sides. 'Do you remember telling me that you would be proud to have a daughter like me?' I asked, timidly, in case he had forgotten.

'Yes, Lucy, of course I remember. It's as true now as it was then. In fact it's probably even truer now as I have got to know you a lot more since then.' As he spoke these kind words to me, I could not help but think that I would have been very proud and indeed very lucky to have had a father like Adam.

Adam told me to snuggle back down and let him finish reading to me. 'Go on, Lucy, relax now and go to sleep. Let me finish reading the story.' I did as I was told. Listening intently to Adam's voice, concentrating only on the soothing rhythm and tone of his speech as he narrated the story of Pooh Bear and Christopher Robin parting forever, I somehow wandered off into a dreamless and unbroken sleep.